A King Produ

Part 2

Genesis & Genevieve...Am I My Brother's Keeper

A Novel

Joy Deja King

ISBN 13: 979-8-9861059-6-3
Cover concept by Joy Deja King & www.MarionDesigns.com
Cover layout and graphic design by www.MarionDesigns.com
Cover Model: Joy Deja King
Typesetting: Keith Saunders
Editors: Suzy McGlown and Raven Douglass

Library of Congress Cataloging-in-Publication Data;
King, Deja Joy
Trife Life 2 Lavish Part 2 Genesis & Genevieve...Am I My Brother's Keeper:
a novel/by Joy Deja King
For complete Library of Congress Copyright info visit;
www.joydejaking.com Twitter: @joydejaking

A King Production
P.O. Box 912, Collierville, TN 38027

A King Production and the above portrayal log are trademarks of A King Production LLC

This Book is Dedicated To My:

Family, Readers and Supporters.

I LOVE you guys so much. Please believe that!!

Dear Readers:

You've followed me on a journey that sometimes can be a bit complex. I have created a variety of characters that I love very much who each have their own story. And with each book I bring them closer and closer together. They all come full circle in the final installment of the Bitch, Stackin' Paper and Trife Life To Lavish series before I begin Bitch…A New Beginning. If you haven't checked out all my books, please do so, as I want my readers to get a full understanding of where it all started. I truly hope you enjoy and thank you for your loyalty and support.

Hugs and Kisses!!

Part 2

Genesis & Genevieve...Am I My Brother's Keeper

"I lick the gun when I'm done, cuz I know that revenge is sweet!"

Rihanna--G4L
(Gangsta 4 Life)

Eye On The Prize
Chapter 1

Arnez stood in the impressive penthouse suite, gazing out the 34th floor view of Times Square. He extracted a Zino Platinum Crown Series Rocket from the sleek metal tube, and then trimmed the end before firing it up with a palm-sized blowtorch lighter covered in silver reptile skin. He exhaled a cloud of smoke as a smile crept across his face.

"It is so lovely to see you again Genevieve," Arnez smirked, admiring the massive billboard she graced in the heart of Times Square. "We have so much catching up to do, since the last time I saw you."

Arnez walked over to the plush white couch in the center of the exotic wood floor and sat down before lifting up his glass of Sassicaia, the great Italian wine off the coffee table and taking a sip. He let out a deep sigh placing his wine glass down and then picked up the manila folder off the table. He opened it up and stared at the pictures of Genevieve that the private investigator he hired had given him earlier in the week. For the first time in months

Arnez had a tangible lead on his prized target and he had no intentions of letting her slip through his fingers.

"Yes, Genevieve, I believe our reunion is long overdue," Arnez said, before depositing his ashes across her face.

"Genesis, if we don't leave shortly we're going to miss our flight."

"I understand that, but I have to wait here for this delivery. Maybe it's best you go ahead without me. I can take a flight out tonight or tomorrow morning."

"I don't want to take the flight without you. We'll wait together." Coco turned away from Genesis as she huffed, not wanting him to see her disdain.

"Finally!" Genesis said when he heard the doorbell. He anxiously made his way to the front door. The FedEx carrier greeted him with a smile and a pen as Genesis signed for the priority overnight envelope. He had practically ripped open the package before the door had completely closed.

"What is that?" CoCo was beyond curious to know what had Genesis' attention so occupied. And for that very reason he either ignored CoCo's question or just didn't hear it because whatever papers he was looking over had his interest on lock.

"This is it! I was expecting so much more...fuck!" Genesis roared, tossing the papers to the floor.

"Are you going to tell me what's going on?" CoCo asked, trying to quickly pick up the papers just in case

2

Genesis decided he immediately wanted them back.

"This private investigator I hired to find my sister and mother said he came across some great information for me. I'm thinking he was close to finding their whereabouts but all this information is from over ten years ago, when they were living in Charlotte, North Carolina. This ain't no recent shit!"

"Wait, Genesis, did you see this?"

"See what?"

"Look," CoCo reached her hand out to Genesis. "When I was putting the papers back in the envelope I noticed this picture, it was kinda stuck in the corner."

"A picture, I was pulling the papers out so fast I must've overlooked it." Genesis took the picture out of CoCo's hand and was silent for a few minutes. He examined every inch of the picture and then turned it over and the names, 'Kevon, Genevieve and Teresa' were written on the back.

"Genesis are you okay?"

"This is my mother and sister. It's an old picture but it's them. Genevieve can't be no more than six or seven, and my mother," Genesis said with a slight whisper to his voice as his finger traced over her face. This must be the man she married," he reasoned, sizing up Kevon.

Genesis sat down on the sofa, clutching the picture. It was the first image he had seen of his family since the last time his mother came to see him at the juvenile facility when Genevieve was only a baby. Having something concrete in his hands once again brought Genesis hope that one day soon he would be reunited with his family and he wouldn't give up until that happened.

"Supreme, we really need to go."

"What…we're gonna miss the flight," he sulked sarcastically. "It's a private jet, they leave when we get there, we ain't on nobodies time but ours."

"They've been waiting for over two hours."

"A little longer isn't gonna hurt."

"Do you not want to go, is that it?"

"Precious, if I didn't want to go, I wouldn't fuckin' go."

"Well that's how you're acting."

"Do you really think I'ma miss Aaliyah's birthday party? Get the fuck outta here!"

"You making it hard to tell by delaying the time we're supposed to be leaving."

"Whatever, I have some shit I need to take care of."

"Fine, you take care of *your shit* and let me know when you're ready," Precious barked back, walking out their bedroom. She was tempted to pick up the crystal vase off the dresser and throw it at Supreme, on her way out but decided against it. Those sorts of volatile feelings had become the norm for Precious in recent months.

Ever since Aaliyah needed a blood transfusion and DNA test proved Nico was her father, it seemed to be war of the roses between her and Supreme. Precious knew that Supreme still loved Aaliyah like she was his own, the problem was she wasn't and Nico made that very clear. When Aaliyah was recovering from her surgery, Nico never left her side. He demanded to play a full-time role in her life and damn near seemed like he wanted to move into the Mills' home or at the very least be their next door neighbor. So Precious had no choice but to come up with a fair and reasonable visitation arrangement that would bring some sort of peace in what had turned into a beyond chaotic environment. With them living on the West Coast and Nico residing on the East Coast it wasn't an easy task but somehow they made it work. Well, Precious and Nico made it work, Supreme was an entirely different story. Precious couldn't fault Nico for wanting to play an active role in his daughter's life but she could also understand Supreme's pain and anger over the entire situation. So she went out of her way to try and appease him. But no matter how hard Precious tried, Supreme seemed determined not to forgive her.

"I still can't believe it's me on that billboard." Nichelle stared in awe.

"Well it is. I said it would happen. I never make a promise I can't keep."

"I'll never doubt you again, that's for sure," Nichelle smiled. Akil walked up behind her and gently massaged Nichelle's shoulders as they both looked out the massive window from his loft apartment.

"I'm so proud of you. I knew I saw something special in you, but I wasn't sure you would allow me to help you bring it out for the world to see but you have."

"I think you're giving me way too much credit."

"I don't think you're giving yourself enough credit.

5

And trust me, this is only the beginning. You're a star, Nichelle. If seeing your billboard plastered in the middle of Times Square doesn't make you a believer then I think what I'm about to tell you now will."

Nichelle turned around and faced Akil with a puzzled look across her face.

"Have you ever heard of T-Roc?"

"Of course, who hasn't? He's a mogul legend in New York."

"You're right. I actually got my start as an intern for T-Roc. He taught me everything I know and then some. He's much more than a legend in New York. His business savvy expands across the world. So when T-Roc reached out to me and said he wanted you to be the face of the new women's fragrance line he's launching, I felt pleased that someone I admire sees the same winner in you that I do."

"Wait, press rewind for a second, did I hear you correctly?" Nichelle's mouth dropped back open waiting for Akil's response.

"Yes, you did. T-Roc wants you to represent his perfume line. Forget about just billboards. We're talking commercials, magazine ads, and national coverage. He's prepared to dedicate a huge campaign budget so this perfume can compete with anybody in this market."

"And he wants me, why? I'm not exactly what you would call polished. Real talk, at the end of the day; I'm just a project girl."

"No, Nichelle, you're so much more than that. But being from the projects, and being able to still exude an innocence although I know you've faced so many obstacles, makes your story that much more powerful. You can inspire so many young girls."

Nichelle shook her head in disbelief with all the good fortune that seemed to be coming her way, virtually overnight. "I don't know Akil. I still can't believe that with all the beautiful women in the world, that T-Roc actually wants me."

"Well, maybe this contract will make you a believer," Akil said, opening up his briefcase. "I reviewed it and to me it's more than fair, as a matter of fact it's very generous. But have your attorney look over it. I believe she will agree." Akil handed Nichelle the papers and her mind instantly began having flashbacks to what her life had been like for the last several months.

It seemed like only yesterday she was running for her life, trying to escape death at the hands of her ex-boyfriend's cousin Arnez. Now she was sitting in Akil's loft, holding a contract worth more money than she ever imagined. No, it wasn't going to make her a millionaire but Nichelle's biggest dream was to one day get a job making fifty thousand dollars a year with benefits.

So much had changed in her life but a lot more had stayed the same. Instead of running, Nichelle was now plastered on a billboard in Times Square which would make most people feel on top of the world. But, Nichelle was miserable and was suffering deep depression. She was doing a wonderful job of hiding it from people but at night she cried herself to sleep. Nichelle still had no clue what happened to her best friend Tierra. The nightmares continued to haunt her, which consisted of hearing gunshots and watching Tierra fall to the ground. Nichelle didn't know if Tierra was dead or alive.

Every time she thought about it, guilt flooded her body. Nichelle felt that she should've done more to help her friend. But in reality there was nothing she could've done. Her desire to go back wouldn't have stopped a bullet from piercing through Tierra. Nichelle did what her best friend screamed out for her to do and that was to run. Nichelle ran through dark alleys and the grimy streets she used to call home. She ran until running out of breath and damn near passing out on the side of the street. That night remained crystal clear in her mind but a lot of what happened next seemed like a blur. That was due to the constant heartache of not only losing her best friend Tierra but also Renny, who she was still in love with. After all this time he hadn't reached out to her and she purposely kept her cell number the same in hopes that one day she would pick up and it would be his voice on the other end of the line.

With all that being said, Nichelle's biggest pain came from the death of her mother and the realization that she had a brother she yearned to reunite with. All Nichelle knew was his name was Genesis and no matter what it took, she would find him.

Regrets

Chapter 2

By the time Genesis and CoCo arrived in New York, the silence between them was about to push her over the edge. She knew Genesis was preoccupied with the picture and information he received about his mother and sister but CoCo felt as if he was shutting her out.

"Do you want to stop by the hotel before we pick up Amir or do you want to go straight there?" CoCo asked, hoping to get some dialogue going between them.

"Actually, I'ma drop you off at the hotel and go pick up Amir myself. I'm sure you're tired anyway."

"Actually, I'm not tired. I want to ride with you. I haven't seen Amir in weeks. I miss him!"

"Yeah, I miss him too. But I think it's best if I go pick him up alone."

"Why? Because you don't want Talisa's parents to see me with you, is that it?"

"I just think it's better if I go alone."

"Genesis, there is nothing wrong with me going with

you, we're friends. And I'm like a mother to Amir."

"Yeah, but you're not his mother." Those words cut through CoCo deeply. They seemed so cold coming from Genesis' mouth. CoCo shifted her body in the car, turning away from Genesis unable to hide the pain he delivered to her. "CoCo, I didn't mean it like that." Genesis said, trying to undo some of the damage.

"Then how did you mean it?"

"I know that you love Amir and in a lot of ways you have been like a mother to him but Talisa's parents don't see it that way. To them Talisa is Amir's mother and always will be. I don't need you all up in their face reminding them that their daughter will never have a chance to know her son."

"I hear you Genesis, but I'm sure Mr. and Mrs. Washington knows that one day you're going to get a girlfriend or get remarried and that woman will be a mother to Amir."

"We'll get to that bridge when it's time to cross it. For now, that's not the case so there is no need to discuss it."

CoCo nodded her head, hip enough to know it would do her no good to try and keep the discussion going. Genesis made his stance clear and for now she had no choice but to accept it. The last thing she wanted to do was alienate him and pursuing what was a dead issue to him would do just that.

"I'll call you when we're on our way back," Genesis said, pulling up to the front of the hotel.

"Cool, I'll see you later on." CoCo got out the car heated, but kept her emotions in check. She would play her position for as long as necessary because in her mind,

Genesis was well worth the wait.

When their private jet landed at Teterboro in New Jersey, Precious was looking forward to seeing her daughter but not being bothered with the drama that was for sure to come with it.

"What time does the party start tomorrow?"

"I think eight or nine, it's a sleepover."

"I still don't understand how Nico got Aaliyah for her birthday."

"Supreme, you know it is part of the visitation schedule. We switch off on birthdays. We had Aaliyah last year and Nico has her this year. It's not like he doesn't invite us to come and celebrate with her, unlike you."

"Are you defending him?" Supreme asked, in an accusatory tone as they stood outside their awaiting limo.

"Can we have this conversation when we get in the car, because it's cold out here!" Supreme continued to stand in position, determined to make Precious answer him. It was evident the limo driver wanted to do his job and open the door but Supreme was blocking that from happening.

"Listen, I'm not defending Nico, I'm simply stating the facts. Last year you ordered Nico to stay away from Aaliyah's party. It wasn't until he threatened to drag us to court for custody that you backed down. Then you gave him the wrong location and time for the party. By the time he arrived the shit was over. But even after all that foolishness, Nico made sure to include us this year for Aaliyah's party, your parents and whoever else we wanted to invite. So stop being so negative about the situation because it could be a lot worse."

"No the fuck it couldn't be," Supreme stated dryly before opening the door and getting in.

During Genesis' drive he kept replaying his conversation with CoCo. He felt that maybe he'd been too hard on her. She had been such a rock for him, especially when it came to Amir. Initially, after Talisa died, it was almost impossible for Genesis to bond with his son. Whenever he would hold him, the pain was unbearable because it was a constant reminder of what he'd lost—his wife. Genesis also felt an enormous amount of guilt that he'd played a pivotal role in Amir losing his mother. CoCo's presence and the love she bestowed upon Amir played a major part in helping Genesis get through the darkest period of his life.

The vibration from Genesis' phone, released him from his thoughts. "What's good," he answered, recognizing the phone number.

"As always everything."

"I wouldn't expect anything less from a major player like you."

"Stop acting like big shit ain't jumping off your way."

"Whatever man," Genesis countered, with a slight chuckle. What can I do for you?"

"I'm hoping I can do something for you and you'll agree to it."

"Oh shit! T-Roc, every time you get to talking like that, you up to no good." Both men broke out in laughter.

"I feel you, but seriously, this is an excellent business opportunity I'm bringing your way. When can I come to Philly and discuss this with you? The sooner the better."

"I'm actually in New York."

"Get the fuck outta here. How you coming to my town and not letting me know."

"It's a short trip. I came to get Amir because a dude I do a lot of business with, is having a birthday party for his daughter."

"Do you think you can squeeze in a meeting with me while you're in town?"

"I'll tell you what. Why don't you come to the birthday party tomorrow, bring the twins. It's supposed to be really nice. And while the kids are playing we can discuss business."

"That's not a bad idea. I'll bring Chantal to make sure the kids don't cause too much trouble while we handling business."

"Who is Chantal, the nanny?"

"No, that's my wife, although now that I think about it, she'll probably want to bring the nanny too. Let's just say my wife isn't really the domestic type."

"Ha, ha, that's funny. I've never met your wife. But bring her and whoever else, I'm sure it won't be a problem. I'll text you later on with the address and time it starts."

"Sounds good to me and I believe you're going to be very pleased with my business proposition."

"No doubt in my mind, I'll see you tomorrow." By the time Genesis finished his conversation with T-Roc he had reached the Washington's estate. No matter how many times he had been there it never got any easier to face them.

13

Promises

Chapter 3

Quentin sat quietly with his body positioned upright and his hands firmly folded. The notched collar; three-button, long sleeve dark navy suit with a single front pleat on his slacks draped his long lean body to perfection. The luxurious texture of the fabric automatically made one say to themselves: made in Italy, without having to investigate the inside of his tag. Yes, Quentin Jacobs's style and grooming was immaculate to say the least, even when visiting a prison.

"Daddy, it's so good to see you," Maya smiled giving her father a hug. He squeezed her tightly, before both sat down.

"You know I always look forward to my visits with you." And Quentin did, as he never missed one. He had been coming to visit Maya on a regular basis ever since she was found guilty and locked up. As he stared in her eyes, he couldn't imagine that a young lady with such an angelic face could be the monster many painted her to be.

"And I always look forward to you coming. Honestly,

I'm constantly afraid that one day I'll get a letter, or one of the guards will tell me that you're never coming back to visit."

Quentin reached for Maya's hand, and rubbed it gently. "I will never disappear from your life again, I promise you."

"Do you mean that?"

"Of course I do! As we sit here I have the best lawyers possible working on an appeal for your case."

"Do you think they'll be able to get the verdict overturned?"

"That's my hope."

"Mine too," Maya said, wiping away a single tear before putting her head down.

"Don't cry. I know it must be torture being locked up like this but you have to be strong."

"I know but it's so hard. My mother only comes once in awhile and although Precious knows that we're sisters she doesn't want anything to do with me. Have you spoken to her for me?"

"No, she doesn't want anything to do with me either. But hopefully when I see her tomorrow I can change her mind."

"Tomorrow, what's happening tomorrow?"

"Aaliyah's birthday party."

"How did you get invited?"

"Nico. He has been very supportive about me having a relationship with my granddaughter."

"I'm sure Precious is not pleased with that. And poor Supreme, he must be devastated that Aaliyah's Nico's daughter. Are they still even married?"

"From what I understand, they're doing everything they can to make it work. But don't you stress yourself about Supreme. He's probably the biggest reason you're locked away in here now. All the lies he fed you, leading you on the way he did. You were young and naive, he took advantage of that."

"Daddy, don't blame Supreme. He didn't mean to lead me on. He really is a good man."

"There you go protecting him again. You still can't see how he manipulated you and the situation to benefit himself. He's even manipulating your sister. I just hope she sees the light before it's too late."

Maya sat quietly with a childlike expression on her face. With her make-up free face and hair loosely pulled back in a high school cheerleader ponytail, it was easy to understand how her father could be swindled by her lies. Convincing was an understatement for Maya's deception. From day one she played the victim with Quentin and it had worked brilliantly. He truly believed that Maya had simply been a puppet for Mike, Devon and Supreme, when in all actuality she was the puppet master.

"It means so much to me that you're in my corner. I promise you, that if I do get out of this hell hole, I will do everything possible to be the daughter you deserve and make you proud of me."

"You will get out and when you do, we will put this nightmare behind you once and for all."

Nichelle was lost in her own world and hadn't noticed

the cab had come to a stop. It wasn't until simultaneously her cell started ringing and the cab driver was asking for his money that she realized they had arrived at the boutique in Soho.

"Just a minute," she said to the cab driver before answering her phone. "Hello."

"I need to see you." Nichelle's heart dropped when she heard the familiar voice.

"Do you have any idea how long I've been waiting for your call?"

"Miss, I need my money!" the driver spewed, speaking in broken English.

"I'm sorry." Nichelle rummaged through her purse, trying to locate her wallet while firmly holding on to her phone. She didn't want to take any chances of accidentally disconnecting from her call. She quickly paid the cab driver and got out.

"Where are you?"

"In Soho, where are you?" There was a long awkward silence. "Renny, after all this time you decide to call me but you can't tell me where you're at?"

"I'm in New York. Can I see you?"

"How long have you been here?"

"I can answer all your questions when I see you. So can I see you?"

"When?"

"How about now, I'm not too far from Soho."

"I have a fitting I have to do right now. It'll probably take a couple of hours."

"A fitting...that's right, how can I forget you're a model now." From the monotone of Renny's voice, Nichelle couldn't tell if he was mocking or acknowledging what her new career was.

"Can you wait until I'm done, or…"

"I can wait," Renny said, quickly cutting her off. "I'll call you back in a couple of hours and we can decide where to meet."

"Okay, I'll talk to you then." Nichelle kept the phone to her mouth for a few seconds longer not wanting the call to end. It seemed like an eternity since she had contact with Renny and hanging up the phone made her afraid that it would be another eternity before she would hear his voice again.

"Genesis, come in," Mrs. Washington said, as he stepped inside their home. Each time he did so, he would have flashbacks to the first time Talisa brought him over to meet her parents. It seemed like life couldn't get any more perfect than it was at that time.

"How have you been?"

"As well as can be expected but having Amir here always makes it better."

"Where is the little fella?"

"He's not so little anymore. But he's outside in the back with Jeffrey. That little boy sure brings out the kid in him. It gives him an excuse to act completely childish," she laughed.

"I know what you mean. I catch myself acting the same way with Amir."

"Yeah, I can't wait to tell Talisa how when we were at the park the other day, Amir grabbed this boy's…" Mrs. Washington's voice trailed off after catching herself. "I apologize. Sometimes I find myself speaking of Talisa as if she's still alive."

"There's no need to apologize."

"Do you know when the doorbell rings I often believe I'll open the door and she'll be standing there, greeting me with her jubilant, wide smile. Nobody had a smile like Talisa's. She could make the gloomiest day bright with her smile."

"I know, you're right."

"Amir has her smile. He has her warmth and loving spirit too." Genesis could see the tears swelling up in Mrs. Washington's eyes and this was the very reason he hated having to see them. Talisa's presence was on full wattage the moment you stepped inside their home. All the work it took for Genesis to suppress his pain from losing Talisa was brought right back to the surface when having to face her mother and father.

"Daddy," Genesis heard Amir scream out, bringing some closure to an uncomfortable moment. Amir ran towards his father and Genesis lifted him up, desperately needing the positive energy that consumed him every time he held his son.

"How are you, Mr. Washington?"

"Well," he said, with a slight nod.

"Amir, don't you want that ice cream sundae I promised you."

"Yes grandpa!"

"Your grandmother is going to take you to the kitchen to get it."

"That's right, now follow me. First one to the kitchen gets a cherry on top." Genesis put Amir down and watched as he tried to beat his grandmother to the kitchen. He was so full of life and unaware of what he'd lost. Genesis couldn't help but think that maybe it was better that way. He would never want his son to feel the heartache that each of them harbored every day.

"Have you come any closer to finding out who murdered my daughter?" Mr. Washington asked, once his wife and grandson were completely out of view.

"No, I'm still working on it."

"I don't believe you're working hard enough."

"Excuse me?"

"It's been how long now, and still nothing! Or do you have so many enemies that you can't decide which one gunned down your wife in cold blood."

"I understand your anger but never question if I'm doing everything necessary to make sure the person responsible for Talisa's death is punished."

"I just know as time passes we can forget about lost loved ones, especially when we replace them with new ones."

"No one will ever replace Talisa. And I promise whoever murdered her will pay the ultimate price."

"I'm counting on that. My daughter deserves justice and you better make sure she gets it. If not, you'll have to answer to me."

Can't I Live
Chapter 4

Nichelle didn't have time to relish in the fabulous outfits she was being fitted for because the only thing on her mind, better yet person on her mind was Renny. There were a ton of questions she wanted to ask him and the sooner they hooked up the quicker it would happen.

"How much longer do you think we'll be?" She looked at the time and the two hour mark had passed. Although Renny hadn't called yet she believed he would and wanted to make sure she was available when he did.

"You have one more outfit to try on and then we're done."

"Cool."

"Were there any outfits that you wanted to keep for yourself?" the perky, extra petite red head inquired.

"No, I'm good but thanks."

"Really? Most of the models that come through here, we have to check their bags before they leave. Never have we had someone turn down free clothes."

"The clothes are cute but this stuff isn't really my style," Nichelle explained, sizing up what appeared to be alien nation inspired threads that were strictly meant to appear on runways and magazine ads, not the streets.

"I totally get it but let me know if you change your mind." Just then Nichelle heard her cell ringing.

"Hold on a minute. I need to get that call!"

"Sure." Nichelle couldn't free herself fast enough.

"Hello."

"Are you finished?" Nichelle let out a deep sigh realizing it wasn't Renny on the other end of the phone. It was Akil. "Are you okay?"

"Oh yeah, ignore the heavy breathing. I'm trying to fight off this headache I feel coming on."

"Maybe it's a hunger headache. How 'bout I pick you up and take you to dinner…" there was complete stillness on the phone. "Nichelle, are you there?"

"Hold on one second, someone's beeping in…, hello."

"Did I catch you at a bad time?" Nichelle couldn't help as a smile spread across her face from hearing Renny's voice.

"No."

"Good, so are you done handling your business?"

"I will be done in about fifteen more minutes."

"Can you meet me at Blue Ribbon in say, thirty minutes?"

"Where's Blue Ribbon?"

"In Soho. I think the address is 97 Sullivan Street."

"Okay, I'll see you there." Nichelle clicked back over to the other line and Akil was still waiting. "Sorry about that."

"No problem, so are we on for dinner?"

"I would but this headache is starting to really creep up on me. I'ma go home and take a couple Excedrin PM and sleep this off."

"Yeah, you do that. I'll call you tomorrow. Feel better."

"Thanks." Nichelle didn't like lying to Akil but there was a part of her life that she kept hidden from him, which included Renny. He knew that she was a young girl from the hood that he pulled out of oblivion. She had confided in him that her mother had died but he was unaware of the circumstances surrounding her death. Nor did he know about her trying to find out what happened to her best friend Tierra and her brother Genesis. Those were secrets Nichelle planned not to ever share with him.

Delondo sat patiently reading the paper at his favorite restaurant, Lacroix at the Rittenhouse. While reading, he briefly thought back to how he almost put the place out of business when he had his men shoot up this very restaurant in his quest to take out Arnez for good. It still angered Delondo that with all the bloodshed, Arnez managed to walk away unscathed that faithful night. But that flaw hadn't deterred him from seeking revenge. He knew it was only a matter of time before he would bring his enemy down for not only trying to destroy his business but for retaliation for his cousin Tonya.

"I was beginning to think you forgot how to tell time," Delondo commented when his worker sat down.

"My fault but one of our spots had a minor problem that I had to iron out."

"Has it been adjusted?"

"No doubt. You know I always stay on top of my shit. Nothing for you to be concerned about, it's handled."

"That's what I like to hear. So what about my other problem that has been causing a major toothache for way too long?"

"I've been on it, but that nigga Arnez must be under a rock. Nobody on the street has seen that cat."

"Trust, somebody has seen him, you just asking the wrong people."

"I've asked everybody in my circle that I trust to keep shit confidential."

"Then you need to expand your circle. Unless that nigga show up dead, he's on the move able to be found."

"I feel you."

Delondo leaned slightly over the table, making intense eye contact with his worker.

"Roscoe, I don't need you to feel me. I want you to bring that motherfucker to me. He's enjoyed freedom way too long and it's time for him to meet his maker."

Even though it was brick outside, Nichelle decided to walk to the Blue Ribbon. Amanda, the lady who had done her fitting told her Sullivan Street was only a few blocks away so she decided to weather the cold air. She also figured it would be quicker since a cab would get caught in traffic and what should take five minutes, could easily turn into a twenty minute ride.

The sounds from the hustle and bustle of people walking the streets and the cab drivers blowing their horns filled the air with deafening noise. The always hectic action one encountered being in New York City could make it sometimes impossible to focus on what was going on around you. It was easy to get caught slipping and Nichelle got schooled to that the moment she turned the corner.

It wasn't until the solid grip of what felt like a man's hand grab the back of her neck did she realize she was in danger. She tried in vain to jerk her body forward to break free but the grasp was so tight that instead of moving away it brought her closer to her assailant. Nichelle couldn't even let out a scream because the angle at which he had grabbed her was practically cutting off her circulation. With the night air and being on a less busy street, it seemed as if everyone was unaware of the peril Nichelle was in. Even as she dangled her feet, trying to get the attention of some pedestrian who might be concerned for her safety, she quickly felt hopeless when she eyed an awaiting dark colored van from the corner of her eye.

Nichelle was no match for the strong goon who was holding her as if she was a one pound rag doll. Right when all optimism had faded and she was about to be tossed in the van, Nichelle heard a car zoom up and then come to a sudden halt. Then she could hear the vehicle speeding up again as it drove closer to them then slowing down, smashing in the back of her attacker's legs, causing him to lose his clutch on Nichelle's neck as the impact brought him to his knees.

Nichelle struggled to get up. She had fallen on top of his body which had protected her from suffering more serious injuries. He screamed out in pain but that wasn't stopping him from trying to get Nichelle back in his grasp.

"Nichelle, are you okay?" Nichelle heard the familiar voice scream out as he ran to her and lifted her off the attacker. He seemed to be somewhat pinned down by the car unable to completely move his body.

"Just get me out of here," Nichelle cried out, locking eyes with her perpetrator before getting in the car. She had never seen him before but by no means would she ever forget his face.

"We should call the police."

"No! Drive and let's get out of here…now!"

Nichelle's hands were shaking uncontrollably as the tires screeched while backing up, freeing her attacker. She saw him still lying on the ground as their car drove off. She put her head down as she tried to fight back the tears. Before she even had time to process what had just taken place her cell phone began ringing. She reached in her coat pocket and answered the phone.

"What happened to you? I've been waiting for twenty minutes."

"You don't know," Nichelle said, in a snappish voice.

"Know what? Nichelle, what are you talking about?"

"So you're not responsible for that piece of shit trying to drag me into his van."

"Hell No! Why would I do that?"

"I haven't heard shit from you in forever and all of sudden you call out the blue wanting to see me. Then while

I'm on my way to meet you somebody grabs me. That's a major fuckin' coincidence!"

"Nichelle, I swear it wasn't me."

"Why should I believe you?"

"Because I know who's responsible."

"Who?"

"My cousin."

"Arnez."

"Yes."

"After all this time, Arnez is still after me, why? What the fuck does he want from me?"

"That's why I need to see you, so I can explain everything that has been going on."

"Does this have anything to do with my brother? Do you know where he is?" Nichelle screamed into the phone.

"I need you to calm down. Where are you? I need to see you."

"I can't see you right now."

Then when, are you okay?"

"I'm fine." As Nichelle began regaining her composure she remembered she wasn't in the car alone. Her fear and anger had her running off at the mouth without thinking of who was in her presence.

"Then when can I see you?"

"I can't talk right now."

"Tell me when I should call you back."

"Later on tonight."

"Okay, make sure you answer."

"I will."

"And Nichelle…"

"Yes."

"Be careful." When the call ended all Nichelle could do was shake her head.

"Now are you going to tell me what's going on?" Nichelle looked over at Akil feeling torn.

"How did you find me?"

"When I was on the phone with you earlier, you didn't seem yourself. I decided to come to the store and give you a ride home. When I got there, Amanda told me you had left a few minutes ago walking to Blue Ribbon. Luckily I observe everything and that van parked the way it was seemed mad suspicious to me. It wasn't until I turned the corner and got closer that I peeped your coat, since I gave it to you and only five of them exist."

"Lucky is right. I don't even want to think about what would've happened to me if you hadn't showed up."

"So what happened? I thought you were going home. Who were you meeting at the Blue Ribbon? I never knew you had a brother."

"I can't deal with your questions right now. Can you please take me home and we can discuss this at another time."

"Is it even safe for you to go home? Nichelle, you need to tell me something. I have a lot of time and money invested in you. And let's not forget, you're about to sign a lucrative deal for T-Roc's perfume line. You're obviously in some sort of danger and I need to take the necessary precautions to protect you."

"Akil, I'm thankful for you saving me a little while ago but right now I'm exhausted and I need some time to soak in what went down."

"Fine, but I don't feel comfortable taking you back to your apartment. You can stay with me tonight."

"I don't want to stay with you. I need my own space right now."

"Then I'm putting you in a hotel for the night and first thing tomorrow, I'm hiring a bodyguard to be with you at all times."

"I don't want a bodyguard."

"You don't have a choice."

Nichelle closed her eyes and knew under the circumstances having a bodyguard would be for the best. If Arnez had tried once to snatch her up, she reasoned he would no doubt try again.

I Will Make It Right
Chapter 5

As Precious loaded the final present in the car, she was so looking forward to Aaliyah's birthday party. It seemed like only yesterday she was holding her daughter in the hospital, thanking God for blessing her with such a beautiful baby girl. Now her daughter was walking and talking with a mind of her own. Precious often wondered where did all the time go, but it seemed a great deal of it was spent apart from Aaliyah and the person she blamed for that was Maya.

Maya had single handedly brought her down, only for Precious to turnaround and return the favor. Precious took great pleasure in knowing that vile snake was sitting exactly where she belonged—in a jail cell.

"Do you have everything?" Supreme's question jolted Precious out of her thoughts.

"Yeah, I'm good. All of Aaliyah's presents are in the car and I'm ready to go."

"Why didn't you have the limo driver do that for you?"

"They weren't heavy, plus I wanted to wrap the presents

myself and load them myself. In a few years Aaliyah won't even care about wrapped presents anymore. When we ask her what she wants, she'll tell us money or credit cards. So I want to savor every moment I can with her being our little girl."

"I never thought about it that way. I guess they do grow up pretty fast."

"Yeah they do. Watching Aaliyah go from a baby to a toddler to now being a little person makes me want to try again."

"Try what again?"

"Having another baby." Precious could see the hesitancy on Supreme's face. "I know things have been shaky between us for awhile now but I think a baby could help us get back to that place we used to be."

"A baby can't save a marriage, Precious."

"But it seems to be able to tear one apart."

"Aaliyah not being my biological daughter isn't what hurt our marriage."

"Really, if my memory serves me correctly that's when shit seemed to go to shambles to me."

"We're already running late. Let's go to the party. We can talk about this later."

"767 5th Avenue at 58th Street," Precious told the driver, as she wondered if there was even the slightest chance she could save her marriage.

"Wow, Nico, you sure went all out for Aaliyah. I mean, damn you got the entire FAO Schwarz for the night. That had to cost you a nice chunk of change," Genesis said, as he scoped the store out.

"It's the first birthday that I've ever done for her and I want her to remember it for the rest of her life."

"I promise you, she'll never forget this shit. Hell, I ain't gonna forget it! Can I be your kid?" Both men laughed, watching from a distance as Aaliyah, Amir and a handful of other kids played together and with the Toy Soldier, Princess and other real life toys.

"I hope we didn't miss the party." T-Roc stated when he walked in with his wife and kids.

"Nico, this is the friend I was telling you about that was stopping by," Genesis said, introducing the two men.

"You didn't tell me a legend was coming through. It's a pleasure to meet you man, I respect your business hustle," Nico smiled as he shook T-Roc's hand.

"I appreciate that. This is my wife Chantal, our daughter Melanie and twins Justina and Justin." The two girls and little boy waved at Nico and Genesis before running off and joining the other kids.

"Your kids are beautiful," Genesis commented.

"Thanks, they're also a handful. Where is your lil' man?"

"Somewhere in that mixture of kids causing raucous."

"What time is the party over?" T-Roc questioned.

"I got the place all night. It's the toy store slumber party," Nico grinned.

"I like that."

"Me too, maybe we can have the twins upcoming birthday party here. They would love it," Chantal chimed in.

"Make it happen then."

"I will. I'ma start working on it right now. I'm sure there's somebody in the store that can assist me. I'll be back." Chantal sashayed off leaving the men alone.

"Man you have it all, beautiful wife; beautiful kids a power player in your field. I congratulate you."

"I appreciate you saying that, Genesis, but there's a lot of stress that comes with it. That's why I'm hoping I can allocate some of it to you."

"I'ma leave you two alone to discuss your business," Nico said politely.

"No need, T-Roc knows we do a lot of business together."

"You can fill me in on it later. I think the Toy Soldier and Princess may need my protection from all those over excited kids. I'll be back in a few."

"Nico seems like a good guy."

"He's the best. We're making a lot of money together. I fucks wit' him hard."

"Hopefully I can interest you in making some more money. More importantly, legitimate money."

"How's that?"

"I'm launching my women's perfume line and I want you to oversee it."

"Man, get the fuck outta here! I don't know nothing about perfume."

"It's not just perfume. I'm combining my music shit with the perfume. You're already a private share holder in my music label I'm giving you an opportunity to play a bigger role."

"How 'bout I don't want to play a bigger role. I like

33

being private, you know, not dealing wit' the bullshit but still collecting a nice fat check."

"Remember you were on the run and I helped you out. You said you owed me, well now I'm trying to collect on that favor."

Genesis glared at T-Roc, puzzled by what he said. T-Roc had never come at him like this and he didn't know how to take it. "What's really going on with you?"

"Real talk?"

"That's all I would expect."

"I believe somebody is stealing from my company and if they're stealing from me then they're stealing from you too since you're a shareholder."

"So what am I supposed to do?"

"Come in and be my eyes and ears. Whoever is doing this is extremely slick and I believe they have help. I don't know who to trust on the inside but I know I can trust you."

"Your trust in me is a good thing but I'm confused. Either somebody is stealing from you or they're not. Is money missing or is it not missing."

"It's not that cut and dry. A couple of deals that should've gone through slipped right through my fingers and a major competitor got them. It was as if they had some inside information on the deals I had put together. Then it appears money is being moved but when I go sniffing around shit seems to miraculously fall in place."

"Are you calling out your people on it?"

"No. I don't want to ring any alarms until I know exactly who is responsible and then they have to deal with me."

"T-Roc, I feel you but what you're asking me to do would require me to move to New York, at least temporarily."

"I know but, Genesis, you're the only person I can trust and who has that street intuition to sniff out the crooks. Plus, you'll be paid a healthy salary. You never know, you might enjoy being a corporate executive."

"I seriously doubt that."

"Genesis, you know if this wasn't important I wouldn't come to you like this. I'm asking for your help."

"I get that and I'm going to give it to you."

"I knew you wouldn't let me down," T-Roc said, giving Genesis a handshake hug combination. "Will you stop by my office on Monday so you can look around and let me introduce you to the top executives? I want you to get a feel for the people you'll be working with and go over the short list of competitors I'm concerned about. Speaking of competitors, the main one just walked in."

Genesis turned to see who T-Roc was speaking of and his eyes first zoomed in on Precious and then to her husband Supreme.

"This really is a small world," Genesis said under his breath.

"I guess you know them."

"Yes, that lovely young lady who is married to Supreme is also Nico's baby mama."

"Hey, Genesis, it's good to see you," Precious greeted him as she walked up.

"You too." Genesis then turned towards Supreme, "glad you could make it." Supreme simply nodded his head acknowledging Genesis.

"Supreme, it's always good to see you. If I knew you'd be here, I would've brought some contracts in hopes we could close some deals."

"I'm sure you would've, T-Roc. But I'm here to enjoy my daughter's birthday party, let's go Precious."

Both men watched as the couple walked off before saying another word.

"I thought you said the birthday party is for Nico's daughter."

"Technically it is. It's a long story but Supreme considers Aaliyah to be his daughter too."

"Oh, kinda how it is with Chantal's daughter with Andre. Although Melanie isn't my biological daughter I consider her to be just as much as mine as the twins."

"Yeah, kinda like that but their story is a lot more complicated, trust me."

"You'll have to give me the details one day. That's one story I would be very interested in hearing."

"I'm sure you would. Oh, there's CoCo," Genesis said, seeing her come in. "You can meet my other partner too."

"That gorgeous woman is your partner and you said I had it all."

Genesis gazed at CoCo as she came towards them. There was no disputing that she always had been and still was a very beautiful and sexy woman. It seemed like no matter what color she wore it glistened against her rich, Hershey chocolate colored skin. And the short shag haircut that only a selected few could rock properly highlighted CoCo's features to perfection. It brought out her wide eyes, high cheekbones and full pouty lips.

"I thought maybe you weren't gonna make it," Genesis commented while giving CoCo a hug.

"The errand I had to run took a little longer than I thought it would. So where's the birthday girl? I have a present for her."

"She's down there playing with Amir and all the rest of the kids."

"I see Supreme and Precious managed to join us for the celebration. I must say I'm very surprised, not so much by Precious but definitely Supreme. It's a good look they came though."

"Yeah it is. CoCo, I want you to meet a very good friend of mine, T-Roc."

"It's a pleasure to meet you."

"Wow, I apologize. I was so busy looking at the kids I didn't even look in your direction."

"No need to apologize."

"Are you kidding me! I've been a fan of yours since forever. I have every CD you put out."

"I haven't come out with my own music in years."

"That's my point. I'm still holding on to it."

"Since I'm no longer making music, I hope you're supporting the artist on my label."

"Of course, I support everything you do. I really am a big fan." CoCo, turned her attention to Genesis and playfully hit him on the chest. "You never even mentioned T-Roc was a friend of yours. You been holding out on me."

"I promise I don't. Honestly, it slipped my mind."

"Whatever!"

"Genesis, you might as well share our good news."

"What good news?"

"T-Roc offered me a job here in New York."

"Doing what?"

"Overseeing his music label and the new perfume line he's launching."

"Really?"

"Yes, I think Genesis would be a perfect fit."

"I see." Genesis could tell CoCo wasn't exactly sold on his new career path.

"No need to be concerned, CoCo, it's only temporary."

"Does that mean you're moving to New York?"

"For a short time."

"Then I guess I'm moving to New York too," she stated as a matter of fact.

"Don't you think it'll be best business wise if you stayed in Philly?"

"Philly is only a couple hours away driving and less than an hour on a flight. And Nico can manage Philly more while we're up here."

"We'll talk about it some more when we get back to the hotel?"

"That's fine. I'ma go see Amir and tell Aaliyah happy birthday."

"Okay."

"My brother, you didn't tell me your partner was in love with you."

"Because I didn't know my personal life was open to discussion."

"We discuss everything else. What's the problem any-way, that woman is fine." T-Roc paused for a moment then followed up with, "Please accept my apology."

"For what?"

"Because I never had the opportunity to meet your wife, I always forget that you were married and became a widower all in the same day. Please forgive me for my thoughtlessness."

"Only if you forgive me for having sordid thoughts about your wife...I kid!" Genesis nudged T-Roc's arm and both men found humor in the comment. Deflating what could have easily become a dark cloud lurking over Genesis' head, allowing himself to sulk in the pain from losing Talisa.

Soldier Of Love
Chapter 6

After the kids relished in their FAO Schwarz fantasy sleepover. Devouring all the ice cream, cake, candy and games they could possibly imagine. They began bringing the excitement down by preparing the little ones for bed with storytelling time.

"Chantal, it's getting late, tell the kids to come on."

"I'm not ready to go," Melanie ran up to them and said.

"Me neither," Justina pouted. "I want to stay for the sleepover. I like Aaliyah, she's going to be my new best friend." T-Roc couldn't help but get a kick out of the things that would come out of his daughter's mouth.

"T-Roc, it would be no problem if your kids stayed. They have plenty of staff and security supervising. Aaliyah's personal nanny is staying the night so your children will be in excellent hands."

"I can vouch for that because I wouldn't let Amir spend the night if I wasn't a million percent sure he was safe."

"I don't have a problem with it, how about you, Chantal?"

"I think it'll be fun for them."

"Yeaaaaah! The girls screamed out together. "Bye mommy, bye daddy," the girls waved running off, brushing past Precious and Supreme on their way.

"Precious, go tell Aaliyah it's time to go."

"Excuse me?"

"I wasn't talking to you Nico, I was speaking to my wife."

"I don't care who you were speaking to, all I know is my daughter isn't going anywhere."

"Can we please not do this," Precious pleaded, knowing things had been going way too smoothly, so with her luck shit was bound to pop off before the night ended.

"Look, we let you have your little birthday party, now it's time for Aaliyah to come home."

"You didn't let me have shit, it's my right as her father to give her a birthday party."

"And you did."

"Well the party ain't over."

"Didn't nobody tell you to rent out the toy store for an overnight sleepover. That was your dumb idea!"

"Yo, get your disrespectful ass outta here," Nico barked, marching towards Supreme.

"Nico, chill! Don't forget there are kids up in here, mainly your daughter," Genesis reminded him, grabbing his shoulder.

"I'll leave but my daughter is coming with me."

"She's not your daughter!"

"Aaliyah is his daughter, and don't you ever say that

shit again!" Precious snarled, making her position clear. "Come on Supreme let's go. We'll be back tomorrow to get Aaliyah. Make sure you have her ready," she snapped at Nico, as they made their exit, before being stopped by one person she dreaded seeing.

"Precious, I hope you're not leaving. I know I'm late but I was hoping to speak with you."

"Quentin, I have nothing to say to you! And now that you're here, I couldn't be leaving at a better time. Now move out my way!" Quentin stepped to the side clearing the path for Precious and Supreme to leave.

"Dare I even ask what that shit was about," Chantal was dying to know.

"How 'bout I tell you over some champagne."

"CoCo, you are speaking my language. Lead the way."

"Genesis, do you all want to come too?"

"You go head. T-Roc and I will meet up with you and Chantal later. Is that cool with you, T-Roc?"

"Yep. Chantal ride with CoCo. I'll call to see where you at when we're on our way."

"Alright baby." Chantal gave her husband a kiss on the lips and hurriedly caught up with CoCo. She was looking forward to hearing all the juicy details of the love triangle gone terribly wrong.

"Nico, you good?" Genesis asked, after the women left.

"Yeah, I just hate that motherfucker. He always tries to ruin some shit. He needs to accept that Aaliyah is my daughter."

"True, but you have to accept that she's his daughter too. Aaliyah is a lucky little girl. She has two fathers that both love her very much."

"True, but that nigga need to show me some respect. He have to deal wit' the fact that I ain't going nowhere... never!"

"Nico, I believe Supreme knows that which is the reason he has such a problem with you," Quentin explained.

"He needs to get over it."

"Maybe in time but enough about Supreme. Where is my beautiful granddaughter? Since my daughter wants nothing to do with me at least I have Aaliyah."

"They're all upstairs listening to a bedtime story. She'll be happy to see you."

"Then let me go upstairs, but Nico, put that Supreme mess behind you. You're a father now, that's all that matters." Those were Quentin's last words to Nico before heading upstairs. Nico felt blessed and proud to have a child especially by a woman he would always love, but that fact didn't change the anger he harbored for Supreme.

"Thank you for what you said to Nico." Those were the first words Supreme had said to Precious since they had left the party. He was completely quiet during the ride back to the hotel and she was beginning to think Supreme was angry with her for leaving and not taking Aaliyah with them.

"I meant it! Nico had no right to say what he did. Aaliyah is your daughter."

"It felt good hearing you say that though."

"Supreme, is that what has been wrong in our

marriage? You didn't believe that I still saw you as Aaliyah's father after the blood test results came back."

"Maybe, I don't know."

"Yeah, Nico might be the biological father but that doesn't change the fact you raised and loved Aaliyah for all that time. You all share a bond that no test can change. In my eyes you are Aaliyah's father. That's not to say that Nico doesn't have the right to be a big part of her life but you're my husband and we're a family."

"Baby, I've been afraid for so long that that wasn't going to be the case but my pride wouldn't let me admit that to you. You and Nico share this history that I'm not a part of and now you share a child together. It's like my family is slipping away."

"Don't you understand I chose you and I will always choose you! Nico is my past. You are my present and my future."

"I love you so much Precious." Supreme hadn't declared his love for her in so long that it brought tears to Precious' eyes hearing him say those words.

"Baby, I love you too. I'll always love you. There isn't another man in this world that will ever have my heart but you." Precious sealed her assertion with a gentle yet passionate kiss that her husband responded to. Supreme pulled her in closer wanting his tongue to first make love to her mouth. He tilted her slender neck back and showered it with kisses. Supreme wanted to take in her scent, the softness of her skin, everything that he had been fighting to no longer crave. He was finally allowing his mind and body to surrender to what he needed more than anything—the love of his wife.

Supreme took his time undressing Precious, appreciating her beauty and the fact she belonged to him. His hands glided down the outline of her body stopping at each curve and spot that deserved special attention. Like her hardened nipples that he wanted to feel inside his mouth. Then he sprinkled her stomach with more kisses as the tip of his fingers played with her nipples, before his tongue stroked her clitoris making Precious weak and no longer able to stand up. Her husband had made love to her entire body without yet entering inside of her with his dick.

Supreme laid her down on the bed as he gazed in her eyes, "I do want us to make a baby together."

"You mean that?" Precious asked breathlessly.

"Every word and I want us to start right now" Supreme said, as he glided his dick deep inside of her letting her warm juices soothe his soul.

Chapter 7

Nichelle's mind was in another world as her attorney was going over the final revisions of her new contract. There were only a few minor details that needed to be adjusted because her lawyer agreed with what Akil had said; the terms were more than generous. But it was difficult for Nichelle to celebrate with all that had transpired in the last forty-eight hours. Renny had reappeared in her life and someone had tried to kidnap her, kill her or both. Then, Renny hadn't called her back which made her suspicious that maybe he was behind the attempted assault. On top of all that, Akil continued to pressure her to tell him everything she knew about what happened that night. Part of her wanted to confide in him but she wasn't ready.

"Nichelle…Nichelle…Nichelle…"

"I'm sorry. My mind was someplace else. I didn't even hear you calling my name."

"Is everything okay with you?"

"Yes, I just have a lot on my mind."

"I could imagine. You're about to be a star."

"Star...I never thought that would be a word someone used to describe me."

"I guarantee you six months to a year from now, a whole lot of people will be using those exact words."

"So I take it everything is complete with the contract?"

"Yes, it's a go! And I feel honored to have been the one to finalize the deal. Thank you!"

"You don't have to thank me, you're a great attorney."

"Nichelle, are you sure you're okay? I mean you're being so calm about all of this. Most women would be jumping off the walls. Running down a list of all the new things they're going to buy with their money."

"Veronica, thanks for your concern but I'm fine. I'm sure once it hits me I'll be doing all those things you were talking about."

"Ok, but if you ever need to talk I'm here and it doesn't have to be just about business."

"Thank you for that."

"I know you're supposed to be meeting with T-Roc so I'm not going to keep you. But try to enjoy yourself, remember you only live once."

"How the fuck did you let her get away, you fuckin' idiot!" Arnez belted.

"Look at me, don't you think I'm just as pissed as you. I'm on these fuckin' crutches."

"Are you whining to me like a fuckin' baby? I don't give a damn about you being on crutches. I was this close to having the bait I needed and you fucked it up!"

"I told you I'm not giving up! I'll get her. I just need a little more time."

"Wait a minute," Arnez shouted before answering his cell. "What can I do for you?"

"I need to see you."

"I'm working on something important so I probably wouldn't be able to get to the West Coast for another week."

"That don't matter 'cause I'm in New York."

"So am I."

"Good, then we can meet right away."

"Sounds important."

"My shit is always important. I'll see you shortly."

When the call ended, Arnez was curious to know what was so important that Supreme needed to see him immediately.

"Nigel, I have some other shit to handle so we'll continue this later. But until then, you concentrate on bringing Genevieve to me. I already had to get rid of two other men because they couldn't get the job done, don't you be the next casualty. Now get out."

"Last night was unbelievable," Precious smiled as she came out the bathroom. "I was hoping you were going to join me in the shower so we could've kept it going."

"I would've loved that but I got a phone call that held me up."

"Nothing's wrong is it?"

"No, but I do have to go meet with someone about some business."

"So do you want me to pick up Aaliyah without you?"

"Yeah, that works. When I'm done I'll meet you at my parents' house. Now let me get in the shower. The sooner I get this meeting over with the sooner I can get back to my beautiful wife and daughter." Supreme kissed Precious and went in the bathroom.

This time yesterday, I thought my marriage was over. Now I'm more in love than ever. Thank you God for helping me save my marriage. Now please let me get pregnant and give my husband the son or daughter he deserves. I know Aaliyah is his child but I need to give Supreme the biological child that I know he truly wants. Please let that happen for us because my family means more to me than anything else in this world.

Precious believed her prayers would be delivered and would do her part to make sure it happened.

Knock...Knock...Knock

Genesis looked out the peephole and saw it was CoCo on the other side of the door.

"How are you this morning?" CoCo smiled, always happy to see Genesis.

"Good, come on in. Sorry I couldn't make it over to the restaurant last night. But after I wrapped things up with Nico and T-Roc I was exhausted."

"No problem, so what do you have planned for today? I was thinking we could take Amir sightseeing."

"You don't know how good that sounds but I have to meet T-Roc at his office. I'm thinking it's going to take up most of my day."

"So you've actually decided to take the job offer. Wow, I thought you were bullshitting but you're serious."

"Very."

"Then I'm serious about moving to New York too."

"CoCo, you don't have to do that."

"I want to do it. Genesis, you can't keep trying to pretend that the feelings I have for you don't exist. Not acknowledging it doesn't make them go away. I'm in love with you. It's as simple as that."

"Nothing in life is ever simple. You know that, CoCo."

"Not when it comes to us I don't, so explain it to me."

"I can't have this conversation with you right now. I'm already running late and I need to go."

"Then we'll talk about it when you get back."

"I'm not sure what time that'll be. It might be late."

"Then I'll wait up." Genesis could see from the look in CoCo's eyes that this was nonnegotiable and decided not to waste any more time with the back and forth.

"That's fine. I'll call you when I get back."

"I'll be waiting," CoCo made clear, as they both left the hotel room.

"Nichelle, it's a pleasure," T-Roc said, standing up from his chair. "Seeing you in person, only confirms what I already knew—you are the perfect fit for my perfume line. You're actually even more perfect than I originally thought." As with most of T-Roc's business decisions, he went with his gut instinct and that included hiring Nichelle without seeing her face to face first. He made the choice strictly off the billboard she graced and her portfolio. There was something raw about her look and T-Roc gravitated towards that.

"Thank you," Nichelle said, putting her head down. Not wanting T-Roc to see her blush."

"Are you shy?" T-Roc questioned in a teasing voice.

"I think your praise is embarrassing her a tad bit," Akil cut in and said.

"I'm fine. But I do truly appreciate you giving me this opportunity. You could've chosen any girl in the world but you chose me. I'll always be grateful to you for that."

"Remember you said that, because when the money and fame starts pouring in, people quickly become ungrateful. I've seen it too many times."

"I can't imagine ever being ungrateful, I've lost way too much," Nichelle said, as her voice faded.

"Repeat that, I didn't catch that last part," T-Roc stated, curious to know what Nichelle had said.

"It was nothing. I just said I'll always be grateful. I promise you that," she smiled.

"And you know what, I believe you. So let's not waste any more time and get to it."

"Sounds like a plan to me. So when did you want to start?" Akil inquired.

"Tomorrow morning, seven a.m."

"Are you serious? I thought you would need more time to plan everything out." Nichelle couldn't hide her surprise.

"My Dear, I've been planning this since the moment I decided to launch my perfume line. The only piece missing—was you. So it's a go."

"Is it possible to be scared and excited all at the same time, because that's what I'm feeling right now."

"Of course, that's only natural. So make sure you get a lot of rest tonight because I want you to shine in front of that camera tomorrow. No dark circles, no fatigue and no being late, are we clear?"

"Yes, T-Roc, we're clear. I won't let you down."

"Good, I'll see the two of you tomorrow."

"No doubt," Akil said as he and Nichelle left T-Roc's office.

"Who was that?" Genesis questioned, catching the back of Nichelle and Akil as they were leaving.

"That was Nichelle, our new spokes model for the perfume line. You'll have a chance to meet her tomorrow morning, when we begin shooting."

"Tomorrow morning is no good for me."

"Why not?"

"I have business with Nico that cannot wait."

"Are you sure?"

"Positive. Taking on this job with you is already gonna squash a lot of time that I need to devote to my business. I know you my boss and all but can you at least grant me some time to tie up some loose ends?" Genesis chuckled, causing a smile to creep across T-Roc's face.

"Since you put it like that, how can I decline your request? But joking aside, would it be so bad to have me as your boss full time? I mean, it would be more so like us working together."

"Are you playing right now or is this a serious question?"

"I'm serious! I mean come on, Genesis. How long do

you plan to stay in the game? I'm offering you a legitimate job where you can make a lot of money."

"Yeah, a lot of money for most people, but nowhere near the type of ends I'm bringing in on this street shit."

"But that's exactly what it is—street shit. You know I have a lot of love for the hustle but when an opportunity knocks to take you out of the streets and still be able to live good, you should take it."

"I feel you but this game is like my identity. These streets define me, the same way sitting behind the desk brokering deals define you."

"Yeah, but sitting behind this desk ain't gonna have me doing 25 to life."

"My Man, I ain't got no plans to do that shit neither… trust me."

"I'm not gonna continue to hassle you about it but think about what I said. The offer is on the table. You never know, these next few months of being my eyes and ears, you might fall in love with a new profession."

"T-Roc, know I appreciate your concern. That's why I'm willing to do whatever you need to see if you have snakes within your camp. But you best believe, once we get down to the bottom of the bullshit, it's back to business as usual for me."

T-Roc knew Genesis meant that shit. Not living a life of crime was like not living at all for a man like Genesis. The streets were his high, his addiction and only a new and powerful high would be able to break him away from it.

53

When Supreme entered Arnez's crib, he only had one agenda and he wasn't leaving until it was guaranteed to get done.

"Supreme, you know I'm always honored by your presence…"

"Cut the bullshit," Supreme barked, interrupting Arnez before he could continue. "I don't have time for no silly ass song and dance wit' you because my wife is expecting me. So let's just get down to it," Supreme said, as he sat down on the sofa with his hands tightly clenched.

"This is your show, tell me what you need."

"Ain't shit changed! What's the holdup with Nico?"

"I'm confused. I thought you put the brakes on that."

"I put the brakes on the hit. But the money I invested in your drug business was supposed to monopolize all the necessary territory to shut Nico down so he would be dried up and dead ass broke."

"At one point it seemed things were moving in that direction but I came across some bumps."

"What sort of bumps?"

"As you know, my main partner, Chanel was murdered. Then this dude in Philly got a major hard-on for me so my moves have to be a little more discreet until I can get rid of his ass."

"What the fuck does any of that have to do with Nico?"

"Because while making smaller moves, Nico has been having a come up."

"And how did you let that happen?"

"From what I understand he linked up with Genesis who has a major connect with this big time cat Quentin.

So right now it's impossible for me to dry him up on the drug game because where they getting their product I can't touch it. But give me some time because I'm working on shutting that motherfucker Genesis down for good. Once I get him, Nico's finished."

"I know all the players you're speaking on and I don't give a fuck about some vendetta you have against Genesis. The only concern I have is getting rid of Nico. If you can't bring him down by eliminating his pockets then the hit is back on and eliminate his life."

"Are you sure you want Nico dead?"

"Hell yeah! If I had that nigga wiped out like I wanted to the first time, then I could've eliminated all the bullshit jumping off right now. I want him out of my family's life—immediately!"

"I'll get my men on it."

"You do that. And don't fuck up Arnez, or you won't see another dime from me."

"Have I ever let you down? It's funny how you seem to forget that it was me that funded your career when you were a struggling rapper in Queens."

"I didn't forget shit. When I wrote you that check with all those zeroes behind it after I blew the fuck up that was payment in full, plus interest and a fuckin' bonus. So if anything, you owe me and don't forget it. Now handle my shit."

Arnez simply nodded and watched as Supreme left. There was no sense in arguing with him because he knew he could never win. Not only was Supreme arrogant and self-righteous, he was also stupid rich. Oh, how the tables had turned in what seemed like such a short period of time. Years ago, before Supreme became a rap phenomenon it was Arnez that was his saving grace.

Arnez was young, rich and hood famous from his rapid come up on the drug scene. One summer when he was making a routine stop through New York, one of his workers told him he had to hear a local kid from the block spit. Arnez wasn't interested as so many people came his way wanting him to fund their grand ambitions. It never amounted to much because everybody thought they were the next great talent, when in actuality, they were the weakest link. But because Arnez's best worker asked him to take a listen he obliged and was willing to give the kid a few minutes of his time. Never did Arnez expect for those few minutes to turn into a few hours.

The moment Arnez walked up to the corner there was a huge crowd of people, boppin' their heads and pumpin' their fist as if at a Jay-Z concert at Madison Square Garden. But you weren't witnessing the evolution of Shawn Corey Carter, but instead the birth of Xavier Mills aka Supreme. When he spit, his flow captured you and wouldn't let go. You were hypnotized and there was no breaking out the trance until Supreme let you go. He had a lyrical gift, there was no denying that and Arnez wanted in.

From that day forward Arnez became the unofficial sponsor of Supreme's career. He funded everything from studio time, his wardrobe to jewelry so Supreme looked like he had signed a seven figure advance even though he was still living in the basement of his parent's house. Arnez had no doubt in his mind that eventually Supreme would rise to the top and be a star but nobody was prepared for how rapidly it happened or the magnitude it grew to be, nobody except for Supreme.

It was as if Supreme had caught a glimpse of his future because as he was coming up he refused to sign paperwork with anybody. Because he was low key and non-confrontational people let it slide not thinking Supreme was being slick. But the joke was on them. He remained a free agent until he finally signed with a label. If Supreme didn't want to, he wasn't legally obligated to give anybody a piece of his pie, but when he hit the jackpot, everybody got paid back plus extra. Supreme knew exactly what he was doing. The people that held it down for him got more than what they were due and he maintained ownership of himself from them.

When Arnez sized up the moves Supreme made, he realized that he was not to be fucked with. When they say bad boys move in silence, Supreme was the perfect representation of that. He knew that Supreme was ruthless and calculating so you could either play by his rules or move the fuck out the way because everybody else would fall down but him.

Chapter 8

Ring…ring…ring

"Hello," Nichelle mumbled in the phone half asleep.

"I need to see you."

"Renny, is that you?" she questioned trying to come out her sleep induced coma.

"Yes. Can I see you?"

"Are you talking about right now?"

"Yes."

"It's three o'clock in the morning," she said eyeing the clock on the nightstand.

"I know it's late but I figured this would be a good time."

"Why is that?"

"Because it's late and it's less likely for someone to be clocking our moves."

"I couldn't get out even if I wanted to."

"Why?"

"Because after what went down last week, there has been a bodyguard with me twenty-four seven."

"Bodyguard…you big time."

"There is nothing big time about having somebody watching you like a hawk."

"Nah, you do need the protection."

"I guess you would know that more than me. What happened to you? I thought you were going to call me later on that night. I'm just now hearing from you."

"Nichelle, there's been so much crazy shit going on. I'm trying to keep our contact limited to protect you."

"Protect me from your cousin. I don't understand what he wants from me."

"It's a long complicated story that I promise to tell you once I see you."

"When will that be?"

"Since you can't see me now, when is good for you?"

"I have a photo shoot in the morning. It'll probably last all day. What about afterwards?"

"Like what time?"

"I'm not sure. Can you call me around four or five? I should have a better idea by that time."

"Cool, that's what I'll do."

"OK, so I'll wait for your call."

"Nichelle," Renny called out as she was about to hang up the phone.

"Yeah."

"I never stopped loving you."

"I've been wanting to hear you say that for so long but how can you love me and leave me like that?"

"Baby, I didn't leave you. If I would've come to you sooner I only would have put your life in further jeopardy.

59

Believe me it was for the best. But I'll explain all that when I see you. Now get some rest. I know you have to get up early but remember I love you."

"I love you too," Nichelle said but Renny had already hung up.

When Genesis got back to his hotel room he was completely exhausted. The first thing he did was lay back on his bed and closed his eyes. T-Roc had pretty much held Genesis hostage once he knew he wouldn't be available to him the next day and now all he wanted to do was sleep. But that didn't seem to be in the plans when he heard knocking at his door.

At first Genesis ignored it but the knocking persisted. "Genesis, I know you're in there, so open the door."

Genesis instantly recognized the voice as being CoCo's. "Hey, CoCo," he said opening the door.

"I thought you were going to call me when you got back?"

"I literally just walked in moments ago, but then you probably already knew that."

"So what you trying to say, I'm stalking you?"

"No, I'm not saying you're stalking me but it seems you know what moves I'm making since you were knocking on my door before I even had a chance to get comfortable."

"I apologize. I guess I might be coming off somewhat pushy but it's only because I feel like you're pushing me away."

"I don't know what you want from me, CoCo. No, that's not right. I know what you want from me but I don't think I can give it to you."

"That's what I don't understand. What's so hard about there being an us?"

"I don't know if I want there to be an us. That's real talk." CoCo put her head down not able to hide her disappointment at what Genesis said. "I'm not trying to hurt you. I'm only being honest."

"I know that you care about me. I'm not crazy, those feelings are real."

"You're right, they are real but I'm still in love with Talisa."

"I get that, Genesis, but Talisa is no longer here."

"Then why do I feel like I'm still married to her." CoCo sat down on the bed unable to come up with an answer to Genesis' question. He was basically telling her he was married to a ghost and how do you compete with that—you can't.

"Let me in, if only for tonight," CoCo stated as she began unbuttoning her shirt.

"What are you doing!" Genesis stood back confused by CoCo's actions.

"I'm not asking for anything besides this one night."

"Then what?"

"We continue on as friends like we always have."

"CoCo, you know this will never work. Once we get in bed together, you'll want more and I can't give it to you."

"I'm a grown woman. I'll deal with it," CoCo said, now standing butt ass naked in front of Genesis. At the end of the day he was a man and CoCo was a bad bitch. She had a waist that looked like it was on crack with an ass that looked like it hadn't missed any meals. And CoCo had the most beautiful chocolate skin he had ever seen. She took his hand and glided it around to the small of her back so Genesis would know it was also the softest skin he had ever felt too.

"CoCo, are you sure you want to do this because I'm not making you any promises."

"The only promise I want from you is to give me your all right now. That's what I need." With that said CoCo placed her lips on Genesis and slowly began undressing him. She wanted to take her time, because she knew this could very well be the first, and last time they would ever make love, and CoCo wanted to savor each moment. As they stood in the center of the hotel room she laid her head on his chiseled chest. She wanted to breathe in the faint scent of his cologne that had not yet faded away.

"CoCo, maybe this is a bad idea," Genesis admitted, trying to use his upper head instead of his lower. CoCo, didn't respond, she quickly knelt down on her knees and swallowed his rock-hard tool, unwilling to give him the chance to stop what she had been yearning for since the first time their eyes met.

CoCo looked up when she heard the low moans of pleasure exhaling from Genesis' mouth. His head was slightly tilted back and as much as she knew he was regretting what they were doing, the satisfaction her wet mouth was bestowing upon him made him bury his reservations in the back of his head. CoCo knew Genesis' biggest concern was that she would fall so deep in love and if he didn't reciprocate those feelings she might become bitter, which would destroy their lucrative business relationship.

When CoCo felt Genesis' dick pulsating in her mouth, she lightly gripped his manhood with her hand, relaxing her jaw, as she pulled away letting her tongue massage his tip upon exit. CoCo stood up still wearing her five-inch metallic sculpted architectural heels. CoCo sprinkled soft kisses down Genesis' neck before whispering in his ear, "Don't think about it, just slide inside of me as if you love me."

Genesis stared deeply into CoCo's eyes and her request seemed simple enough because he did have a lot of love for CoCo and that's why he didn't want to hurt her. But instead of debating the pros and con of the situation Genesis focused on the now. He was willing to give into what they both wanted, which was each other. Genesis caressed the side of CoCo's face before scooping her up and laying her across the bed. The glow from the moon and stars piercing through the massive window highlighted CoCo's voluptuous silhouette. Genesis gazed over each curve and wondered for a quick second if he could not only love CoCo but actually fall in love with her. But without further deliberation, Geneis slid inside her warm juices taking pleasure in the present.

"Are you sure that's her?" Arnez asked Nigel as he sat in the back of the black SUV.

"Yes. I triple checked before I brought you to her."

Arnez watched as the woman left her condo in midtown Manhattan and got into the awaiting car service.

"She definitely looks the part of a professional corporate woman," Arnez commented.

"I'm telling you, that is her. I wouldn't waste your time if I wasn't a hundred percent sure," Nigel reassured him.

"You better not be. You already have one strike against you. You know what they say about three."

"Yeah, I do and I have no intentions of finding out what my three strikes you're out would be. I told you I'm going to deliver and that's what I'll do. This woman can help make it happen."

"Well don't just sit here, follow the car," Arnez directed.

When Arnez saw the car the woman was in come to a stop he decided to make his move. "I'll be back," he said before getting out the SUV and heading across the street. The woman worked in New York's largest central business district so it was easy for Arnez to pretend he was another power player on the move. Of course he always looked the part and in reality Arnez was a power player, only his money wasn't made legitimately.

"Excuse me," Arnez said, as he purposely bumped into the woman, knocking the folder she was holding out of her hand, as they both entered the prominent skyscraper building.

"This is just great! What a moron," she huffed with annoyance under her breath as her important documents spread across the entrance floor.

"Again, I apologize. I was in a rush trying to make this meeting and I wasn't watching where I was going. Let me get this for you."

"That's okay, I got it." They were both on bended knee gathering up the documents and Arnez reached at the same pile of papers as the woman so his hand could brush up against hers. The smoothness of his hand made her make direct eye contact with him for the first time. She was curious to know what man was the owner of the hands that felt as if they had never done manual labor in their life.

"I think this is it," Arnez said, handing the last of the papers to the woman.

"Thank you. I'm sorry if I came across uncouth. Mornings are always hectic for me."

"No need to apologize, I bumped into you, remember," Arnez smiled, oozing with the signature charm he knew how to turn on and off at his convenience.

"Thanks again, but I really must be going and I know you do too."

"Excuse me if I'm crossing the line, but I don't see a ring on your finger. How about you let me make this little incident up to you and let me take you to dinner."

The woman looked down for a moment and then back up with a look of confusion, as if she was surprised the man standing in front of her was asking her out on a date.

"I guess that's a no?" Arnez said, with a look of disappointment on his face.

"Yes, I mean no," she let out a giggle. "What I'm trying to say is no to what you just said, and yes to having dinner with you.

"Wonderful. I'll call you later on so you can tell me what is good for you."

"That sounds great. Here take my card," she said reaching in her purse and then handing Arnez her business card.

Arnez glanced at it, "Veronica, that's a beautiful name and you're an attorney, smart and beautiful…just my luck."

"Thank you. Well, now I'm running late. I have to go."

"I understand. I'll call you later."

"I'm looking forward to it," Veronica smiled as she headed towards the elevators.

Not as much as I am. Arnez was looking forward to getting to know Veronica. She was not only easy on the eyes but he was hoping she would also be a valuable tool in his plot to snatch up Genevieve. He was tired of playing cat and mouse with her and he prayed an inside connect would end this chase once and for all.

When Nichelle arrived on set, they immediately put her in hair and makeup. She welcomed it as it gave her time to think about Renny. She was surprised but elated that he had finally called her again. She was beyond looking forward to seeing him and it wasn't just because she had so many questions she knew he had the answers to. It was also because she missed him terribly. There hadn't been a day that went by that Nichelle didn't think about Renny. Sometimes when she was alone, for hours she would fixate on what he was doing and who he was doing it with. Thoughts of Renny would consume Nichelle and she knew it wouldn't stop until she saw him again.

"You look incredible." The masculine voice jerked

Nichelle out of her thoughts.

"T-Roc, I didn't even see you come in."

"That's to be expected since your eyes were closed," he teased. "But you really do look incredible."

"I wish I could see." There wasn't a mirror in front of Nichell and she was anxious to catch a glimpse at the magic they had created, because that is what great hair and makeup people were able to accomplish. She had witnessed them turn the most average of chicks into cover-girl ready. Watching the transformation was one of the most amazing things ever.

"You will shortly. Are you ready to get in front of the camera?"

"Yeah, I'm a little nervous but I'm ready."

"Don't be nervous, but so you know we're using a Siberian Bengal Tiger in some of the shots."

"Really? I had no idea!"

"I meant to tell you when I saw you yesterday but it slipped my mind. But you've done it before. I actually got the concept from your billboard with the Black Panther. That shit was official. I thought it would be amazing to carry it over with the perfume ad."

"I have to agree, that is a hot idea."

"I think we will all be pleased with the final product. All I need is for you to bring the fire and we're good."

"Don't worry, I'll deliver on my end."

As they put the final touches on Nichelle, her mind started racing on what she would do once the shoot wrapped up for the day. Her bodyguard was basically glued to her hip and she didn't know how she could get rid of him. Nichelle needed private time when she met with Renny and she didn't want Akil or anybody else to know where she would be. She had to come up with something and reasoned she had about eight to nine hours to do so.

"Baby, when are we going back to LA?" Precious asked when she woke up in Supreme's arms.

"I still have some business to handle here, so it's going to at least be a few more days. I hope that's okay with you?"

"You know I'm an East Coast girl by heart so that's cool with me. Do you have business to handle today?"

"As a matter of fact I do. I need to get up so I can get out of here."

"I think I'll take Aaliyah to Central Park. It's supposed to be a beautiful day."

"That'll be a good look. I'll call you later on." Supreme kissed Precious on the lips then went into the bathroom to take a shower.

"Good morning, Mommy," Aaliyah grinned as she ran into the room to get in bed with Precious.

"Hi, baby! Guess where we're going today," she said tickling Aaliyah as she tried to hide under the covers."

"Where?" she asked between loud laughs.

"To Central Park!"

"Can I eat ice cream?"

"Yes, and we're even going to go on a carriage ride."

"With the horses," Aaliyah's eyes beamed.

"That's right. We're going to have so much fun!"

"Can we see daddy Nico too?"

"We'll see, baby."

"Pleaaase," she pleaded with begging eyes.

"Of course, I'm sure your daddy would love that."

"Yeaaaah," Aaliyah clapped her little hands together and all Precious could do was smile.

"Yo, I didn't think you was going to be able to make it today for this meeting," Nico said, when he opened the door to let Genesis in.

"I told you I was coming!"

"Yeah, but that was before you got promoted to a senior level executive position."

"Nigga, you got jokes! Quit wit' all that."

"I'm only speaking the truth. T-Roc might've put his foot down and said no playing hooky today."

"Nico, I get it. Enough of the jokes we got real business to handle."

"True indeed, so let me get right to it. You know that territory in Philly we can't seem to break into?"

Genesis nodded his head, acknowledging he knew what Nico was speaking on.

"After diligently trying to get to the bottom of that shit, come to find out there's this dude that got that motherfucker on lockdown something pretty."

"Just one cat?"

"Yep."

"How is that?"

"From what I understand his prices are ridiculously good."

"What about the product?"

"That's the thing, I heard it's semi and it definitely can't fuck with our shit."

"So what you wanna do? 'Cause Philly is a pretty piece of property that I want back in on. If that Fed shit hadn't happened, all of Philly would be mine."

"You right. But this nigga done came in and shut the shit down. From what I understand that's a major reason that cat Arnez had to get ghost."

"Yeah, Arnez ghost for many reasons. You know I believe he's responsible for the death of my wife."

"What!" this was the first Nico had heard of this. Genesis rarely ever spoke of his deceased wife. He assumed she was off limits and he respected that.

"Yeah, I don't have no proof just my instincts. She was involved with him before me and once she broke it off he became obsessed. He tried to have me murdered but instead got my best friend killed. I can't wait to get my hands on that dirty bastard. But he got to be the slickest moving motherfucker I know."

"How you think that is? It take a lot of money to stay on the move like that."

"That nigga got some money. I'll give him that. He always kept long paper. But with him getting ran out of Philly, and us having ATL on lock, I don't know where his stomping grounds are now. No doubt he making moves somewhere though."

"That's interesting, but all snakes come slithering out sooner or later."

"Damn right, and I'll be right there ready to take his ass

out unless somebody gets to him first. But back to Philly, what you wanna do?"

"What I don't want to do is force our way in. The last thing we need to start is a street war."

"I agree with you on that."

"Good."

"But we still need a way in. What options do we have?"

"We know for a fact that the quality of our product kills his. I was thinking we make him an offer that he can't refuse."

"Which is?"

"We give him an even lower rate. I mean we can afford it. With the price we get from Quentin, we would still make a profit."

"So basically, we're buying our way in?"

"Exactly but everybody profits. He gives us a prime piece of property and we give him better product at a cheaper price that he can make an even higher turnover rate on."

"He can't beat that. When do you plan on hitting him with this proposition?"

"I got one of our dudes working on it right now. The nigga Delondo keeps a low profile. But our guy is cool with his right hand man Roscoe. Once he sets up the meeting, it's on."

"If you can, try to get the meeting here in New York. With this shit I'm doing with T-Roc, it might be kinda hard to get to Philly."

"Yeah, yeah, yeah…I know you working a nine to five, nigga. I got you!"

"Here we go with the jokes again."

"Wait, hold on a sec, this Precious calling me. What's up?"

"Hey, are you busy?"

"Why what's going on?"

"We were in the city and Aaliyah wanted to see you. But I totally understand if you're busy."

"I always have time for my daughter. I didn't know you all were still in town."

"Supreme has some business to handle, so we're staying for a few extra days."

"OK, well I would love to see Aaliyah."

"Are you at your house in Jersey, or are you at your apartment in the city?"

"I'm at the crib in the city."

"Cool, that works out good then."

"Are you on your way now?"

"We're about to get some ice cream, we'll come over after that."

"I'll see you soon."

"So your baby mama coming to see you?"

"Now you got jokes!"

"Yeah I do," Genesis laughed. "But I'm glad to see that somehow you all are making this work. 'Cause this is no doubt a sticky situation."

"Who you telling and if Supreme don't learn to accept me as Aaliyah's father it's only going to get stickier."

Knock...knock...knock

"Is that Precious already?" Genesis wondered out loud when he heard the knocking at the door.

"No, that's probably Quentin. I told him to stop by

if he had a chance because I wanted him to be in on the whole Philly situation. Being the greedy motherfucker that I am, I'm hoping we can talk him into giving us an even better rate on the product to makeup the major discount we hitting Delondo with."

"Shit, I feel you. It don't hurt to try. You go speak with Quentin, I need to take this call," Genesis said, going to the back for some privacy. "Hello."

"Hey, you were gone when I woke up this morning and I wanted to see how you were doing."

"Yeah, I had to meet with Nico about some business."

"Is there a reason why you didn't want me there?"

"Because some of my Philly business doesn't have anything to do with you. You know that a few of the deals I'm involved in are strictly partnered with Nico, this is one of them."

"True, but I thought that since you're going to be heavy in New York for a minute you would want me to play a more intricate role with your dealings in Philly."

"You're right, and if I need you I'll pull you in."

"OK, let me know."

"I will…but listen, I'm 'bout to leave here in a little while, do you want to meet for lunch?"

"I can't, I actually have a few things I need to handle. What about an early dinner?"

"That works. Call me when you're ready."

"Got you."

"Oh, and CoCo."

"Yes."

"Last night was amazing."

"I thought so too, see you a little later, bye."

Genesis got off the phone with CoCo relieved that they were still able to discuss shit. At first he felt somewhat awkward but realized it was his mind playing tricks on him. CoCo was able to come at him on some business shit even though they had stepped over the line to personal by becoming intimate. If they could maintain both types of relationships and also keep them separate, Genesis felt that could potentially be the ideal situation for him.

Chapter 9

"Hello," Nichelle's insides filled with excitement when she saw the private number pop across her cell phone screen. She knew it had to be Renny since every time he called the number came up private.

"Hey, did you finish yet?"

"We're wrapping up now."

"How long do you need before you can get outta there?"

"Not much, I just have to find a way to shake off my bodyguard. Where do you want me to meet you at?"

"Come out front."

"You're there now?"

"Yep, I'm on the corner in a black Range Rover."

"How did you know where I was?"

"I always know where you are. So come on. I'm waiting for you."

When Renny ended the call, Nichelle stared at her phone thinking about what he just said; *I always know where you are. Has he been watching me or having somebody watch me? If so for how long?*

"Nichelle…Nichelle…Nichelle!" Akil said louder trying to get Nichelle's attention.

"Akil, what are you doing here," Nichelle said snapping out of her thoughts of Renny.

"I told you I was coming back. But clearly your mind is somewhere else, so you might've forgotten."

"Yeah, I do have a lot on my mind."

"Like I told you before, I'm here if you wanna talk."

"I know and I appreciate that."

"T-Roc said everything went great today, how do you feel about it?" Akil asked, changing the subject. Nichelle's body language was screaming to switch direction of the conversation.

"Beyond amazing! Everybody was so patient and treated me like I was some sort of star."

"You are a star."

"No I'm not. But the fact they made me feel that way speaks volume about their professionalism. It made me work harder to deliver. I didn't wanna let anybody down."

"You didn't and won't…I can promise you that."

"Thanks, you always try to make me feel good and that means a lot to me."

"Well then how 'bout we go and celebrate. Let's cheer to your first official day on the job."

"Not tonight, maybe tomorrow."

"I understand, you're probably exhausted from your long day here."

"Yeah, I am."

"Okay, I'll have Clarence take you home."

"He really doesn't need to do that. It would be nice to have some alone time, if for this one night."

"I can't do that, not after what happened."

"That was weeks ago. We haven't had any problems since."

"Yeah, probably because they see you've been walking around with a three hundred pound killing machine."

"Listen, Akil, just let me have this one night alone. I feel like a prisoner!"

"I can't take that type of chance. A lot of money is being invested in you. To take a careless chance and something bad happen to you is out of the question."

"Fine. Have Clarence bring the car around, while I go to the bathroom."

"OK. I'll come get you when he's ready."

"Thanks." Nichelle watched as Akil walked to the back to get Clarence. When he was out of sight, she quickly gathered her belongings together and made a discreet exit.

"Hi daddy," Aaliyah grinned when Nico answered the door.

"What's up, superstar! Give your daddy a kiss," Nico smiled lifting Aaliyah up in the air.

"What is he doing here?" was the first question Precious asked when she walked through the door and saw Quentin sitting down on the sofa.

"It's grandpa," Aaliyah yelled. Nico put Aaliyah down and she ran to Quentin.

"Precious, don't make a scene," Nico warned.

"Excuse me?" she barked back.

"Aaliyah is here. You don't need to show out in front of her," Nico said in a low but stern voice.

"Fine," she smacked, knowing that Nico was right but pissed all the same.

"Aaliyah, your daddy has a game he wants to play with you while I go talk to your mother."

Precious opened her mouth to say, *No the fuck you not*, but stopped when Nico gave her a threatening look.

"Baby, go play with your daddy, but mommy has to make a stop, so I'll be back."

"Okaaaay, see you later," Aaliyah waved.

"Precious, wait!" Quentin called out, trying to stop her before she left.

"I'm trying to keep my cool because my daughter is here but I don't have shit to talk to you about!"

"How about you just listen then."

"Listen to what…a bunch of bullshit. Please save that for your other daughter."

"At least you're acknowledging I'm your father."

"What do you want from me, Quentin?"

"Just hear me out. You've never given me more than thirty seconds of your time. Would it kill you to give me twenty minutes of your time? I really need more, but I understand this is a work in process."

"Fine, start talking because all you have is five."

"How about we step outside, go for a walk."

"Have it your way because this is going to be a very short walk."

While standing in front of Nico's building, the cool breeze hit Precious' face sending a peaceful chill through her body. The crisp air and beautiful sunny skies almost made her forget that she was standing next to a man she completely loathed.

"I know that you hate me," Quentin began as if reading Precious' mind. "But I believe if you hear my side, you might not be so unforgiving."

"I doubt that seriously, but I said I would give you five minutes so you better get to talking because your time is quickly running out," Precious said eyeing her watch.

"Your mother was breathtakingly beautiful and believe it or not I was in love with her. I believe she loved me too but she loved the drugs more."

"So you were in a real relationship with my mother?"

"I'm not going to lie to you, Precious. I was married at the time that I met your mother. But I was greedy and wanted her to be mine. The circumstances were wrong but yes, the relationship was very real in every sense of the word"

"So what went wrong, why didn't she want you to know I was your daughter?"

"When I met your mother, she was a party girl but only a casual drug user. We use to have a lot of great times together. As my feelings grew deeper, I slowed her down. I knew I couldn't leave my wife, we had a family, three small children but I also wanted your mother in my life. So I put her up. I guess you can say she became my official mistress."

"Your mistress...wow, this is interesting."

"I wasn't perfect and I'm still not. All I want you to

know is the truth before you judge me and turn your back on me."

"Continue."

"For a period of time your mother was content but she was a firecracker—like you. She got restless being a kept woman. I stopped letting her run the streets. The only life I wanted her to have was me. I was a selfish man, Precious. It didn't take long for her to start rebelling against me. She would get missing for a few days, I couldn't find her. I believe during this time she started using again. We would fight then make up. She hated the fact that I wouldn't leave my wife and I couldn't blame her. I was married to somebody else but wanted to own her too."

"I can't believe how real you're keeping this. Honestly, I thought my mom was one of your ho's or something that you knocked up and then tossed to the side when you found out she was pregnant."

"Hell no! I loved your mother as much as I knew how to love any woman."

"So how did it end?"

"One day when I came over she was gone. She didn't come home that night. I thought once again she was upset trying to get payback. But then that night turned into a few days, and a few days turned into a few weeks. By that time I had everybody looking for her. It was known in the streets that she was my woman and I wanted her back home immediately. But no one could locate her. Your mother disappeared. I almost went crazy looking for her."

"And you could never find her?"

Quentin let out a long sigh before continuing. "Yeah

over a year later, she was back on the scene. I had no idea she gave birth, especially not to my child. When I saw your mother again, she was in a whorehouse turning tricks and was a complete junky. My heart broke that day and it has never completely healed."

"Why didn't you save her?"

Quentin paused in the middle of the block and stood directly in front of Precious. His face was solemn and his eyes full of grief. "Don't you think I tried? But I had done my dirt long enough on these streets to know you can't save anybody that doesn't want to save themselves. Your mother didn't want to be saved. I couldn't compete with the high she got from doing drugs and that killed me."

"So what about me? You never saw or knew she had a baby and put two and two together?"

"No, because your mother was never with you. Precious, you're a smart girl. If you think back I'm sure you can remember that your mother was probably hardly ever around."

Precious didn't need to do much thinking back because she knew what Quentin was saying was true. Precious remembered being left with anybody and everybody. There wasn't any sort of stable childcare in her life until Ms. Duncan. All she could do was put her head down and think about the what if's. What if Quentin had known she was his daughter, could he have saved her from the miserable childhood she suffered? Could the love from her father have made her kind-hearted and not so cold? Those were questions she would never be able to answer.

"I'm glad you told me this but it doesn't change our

relationship because I don't know you. You weren't there for me. Maybe that choice wasn't given to you but I'm a grown woman now and it's too late for us."

"No it's not. I refuse to believe that. Just because you're grown doesn't mean you've stopped being my daughter."

"Why is it so important to you for us to have a relationship? You have other children, it's not like I'm the only one."

"You and Maya are my only girls and Precious, when I look at you, you really do remind me so much of your mother. Remember the first time I saw you with Mike. I told him how you reminded me of a woman I used to know a long time ago. Little did I know she was your mother. All I want is the chance I was denied and that's to be a father to you."

Precious couldn't front, Quentin was getting to her. It wasn't just his words but how genuine they sounded. Precious was a master manipulator in every way and nine times out of ten could spot when someone was trying to pull the wool over her eyes but she was getting none of that from Quentin.

"I believe you."

"Do you mean that?"

"I wouldn't have said it if I didn't."

"Then are you willing to try and give us a chance at having a father and daughter relationship?"

There was an extended period of stillness. The atmosphere was only filled with background noise as no words were being spoken between the two. The air almost became haunting as Quentin's powerful stance seemed ready to force Precious to utter a word and break the silence.

"Yes."

"Yes, what?" Quentin inquired moving closer towards his daughter.

"Yes, I wanna try and have a relationship with you. I don't know what's going to happen but I wanna see."

When Quentin wrapped his arms around Precious she was completely stunned. It was unexpected but somehow it felt right. "I'm going to do my best to make up for all our lost time. You're my daughter and I love you."

Tears welled up in Precious' eyes. It wasn't until right then, she realized how much pain had been bottled up inside of her for all those years. It had been too painful for her to admit she wanted and needed the love of her father because it seemed totally out of reach. But now there was a chance and her heart welcomed it.

"I'm very pleased that you accepted my dinner invitation," Arnez said staring at Veronica who was sitting directly across the table.

"You say that as if you're surprised I agreed to come."

"Honestly, I have to admit, I am. A woman like you having dinner with a man like me."

"A man like you...I don't get it. From where I'm sitting, looking at you, I doubt you have a shortage of women friends."

Arnez slightly chuckled and put down the glass of wine he had in his hand. "No shortage but how about quality, you seem to be a very successful lawyer. I've never had an opportunity to have dinner with a woman like that."

"Well you seem to be very successful yourself," Veronica paused for a moment glancing around the restaurant with its vast, vaulted gilded ceilings and mosaic tile floor, from the original nineteenth century design. But the absolutely stunning place was further complimented by a dash of futuristic twenty-first century interior design with picturesque views of St. Patrick's Cathedral and The Palace Courtyard. "You certainly couldn't afford to take me to a pricey place like this if you weren't doing pretty good."

"Who said I was paying. I thought this dinner was on you," Arnez cracked, causing a huge smile to spread across Veronica's face. "But seriously, I'm honored that a woman like you would want to have dinner with me. I didn't think I was your type."

"And what type are you?"

"Let's just say I'm a bit rough around the edges."

"You look anything but rough to me. But since we're being honest, when you first asked for my number I was rather shocked. I didn't think I was exactly your type."

Arnez raised an eyebrow waiting for her to continue.

"I picture your type being more of the bombshell beauty."

"I don't know the last time you looked in the mirror but you're beauty personified."

"Thank you, but I'm not the obvious beautiful that I would think you'd be attracted to."

Arnez leaned back in his chair and grinned. He understood what Veronica was saying but she was exactly how he liked his women—from her shoulder length chestnut brown bob, classic features and voluptuous toned body. She had understated sophisticated beauty that was timeless. From pure visual perception, Veronica was the type of woman that brilliant men like President Obama would gravitate to. But he highly doubted that Veronica had the psychological savvy of a Michelle to marry her own Obama and Arnez's assessment was dead on point.

As competent and fierce as Veronica was when it came to legal terms and contracts she had no self control when it came to the men in her personal life. With all the education she had under her belt, the only type of men she would let under her skirt was criminals. So although when she met Arnez he told her he was on his way to a meeting her gut screamed he was involved in illegal activities and profitable at it. She had dealt with enough of them to know the telltale signs.

"How about we leave here and I show you just how attracted I am to you."

"Excuse me," Veronica choked.

"You heard exactly what I said. Are you coming or are you staying?" Veronica was shocked by the proposition Arnez was making but also very turned on which he knew. Still, Arnez wasn't a hundred percent sure she would take the bait but working with limited time he felt it was best to play his best poker hand now. "Waiter, can you bring me the check. I'm done here. Unless of course you're staying," he turned to Veronica.

"No, I'm done too."

This is going to be fun, Arnez thought to himself as he stood up and walked to the chair Veronica was sitting in and took her hand. She willingly gave it to him as they left.

Nichelle stood on the corner quickly looking around in all directions. She wanted to make sure that Akil hadn't followed her out and she was also searching for any sign of Renny. She was discreet with her departure but there was also that chance she wasn't discreet enough. After not seeing Renny she grabbed her cell to call him but quickly realized she had no number on him. Then a quick flash of light caught Nichelle's attention and she turned her head to see a flicker of high beam lights coming from a dark colored Range Rover. Her heart began rapidly beating as she walked towards the Range and it slowly drove closer to her. When it stopped near her, she still couldn't see inside because of the dark tint. That didn't stop Nichelle from walking closer and reaching for the passenger side door handle. When she opened it this rush of emotions flooded her. She hadn't seen Renny in what seemed like a lifetime but the love she had for him was more intact than ever.

"Are you getting in?" he asked in the same calm, cool and collected voice that was his signature style. Nichelle got inside and closed the door. As Renny drove off she saw Akil come out the building, looking around as if in a frantic. Then he began blowing up her phone. "Seems like someone is really trying to get in touch with you," Renny commented.

"Yeah, it's somebody I work with," she answered casually, putting her phone on silent. Nichelle knew that Akil was going to be worried sick thinking that somebody snatched her up, so she felt the least she could do was send him a text letting him know she was okay. She would deal with the heated lecture he would no doubt blast her with, when she saw him again in person.

"I missed you," Renny turned towards Nichelle and admitted.

"I missed you too."

"I didn't realize just how much until seeing you again. Those billboards don't do you justice."

"Really…I thought they actually did me too much justice. They have me without one flaw which of course is impossible."

"I'm not talking about that. Those pictures don't show the innocence in your eyes that I see so clearly when you're right here next to me."

"That's ironic, because with all I've been through the past couple of years I don't feel so innocent anymore. From Carmelo and my mother getting killed, seeing Tierra get shot and you leaving me, I think the better word to describe me is damaged."

"You're not damaged and I didn't leave you, you left me—remember."

"Did you really leave me a choice? Our entire relationship was built on lies."

"Us being in love wasn't a lie."

"Then what took you so long to come back for me? You never even called me."

"I was trying to protect you, Nichelle."

"You keep saying that but never explain how. I'm here, in front of your face now. Tell me exactly what was going on and why is your cousin Arnez so determined to get his hands on me?"

When Renny came to the red light, he stopped and stared at Nichelle. "Can we get into that later?"

"No! I've waited long enough. I have to walk around with a bodyguard twenty-four-seven because of Arnez. I don't even feel free, it's like I'm a child. The least thing you can do is tell me why. I also want to know what happened to my best friend. It was like I lost both of you at the same time."

Renny put his head down, and then looked back up when the light turned green, continuing to drive. "Nichelle, I never wanted things to end up like this for you but a lot of times we have no control over what happens in our lives. Please believe I had nothing to do with that bullshit scheme Arnez concocted. When I found out, I tried my best to protect you. That's why I sent Tierra to go get you, but things didn't work out the way I hoped."

"How did you find out what Arnez was up to?"

"I started putting shit together. After we had dinner at his crib that time, a few days later he started asking me a few questions about you. I didn't think too much of it. The business we're in, and the fact he knew we were serious, I figured he wanted to do a little checking around, looking out for my best interest. Then he started asking questions about where you grew up, your mom, and I made the mistake of telling him where she lived. I swear Nichelle, I had no idea he planned on even talking to your mom, let alone killing her."

All Nichelle could do was shake her head. Replaying all this over again was bringing tears to her eyes. But she wanted to know exactly what happened; she needed to know in order to bring some sort of closure to all the chaos. "So how did you finally put it all together?"

"I had to meet Arnez at this safe house and I got there earlier than planned. I heard noises coming out this back room and when I went to open the door to see what was going on, it was locked. Chanel told me that Arnez was in there handling some chick that worked for him who had stolen some money and drugs. So I went outside and made some phone calls and told her I would be back when Arnez was finished."

"Were the noises you heard coming from that room, my mother?" Nichelle asked in a horror stricken voice.

"Yes, but it wasn't until she was already dead I found out. About twenty minutes later, Arnez came out and said an emergency came up and he would need to reschedule our meeting for the next day. Then I saw one of his workers carrying out a covered up body and putting it in the trunk of a car. Then Arnez and Chanel got in another car and drove off. I went back inside to get something I left. I don't know if it was curiosity or a bad feeling but I went back in the room where I heard the noises coming from."

"What did you see?"

"Are you sure you want to know?" Renny questioned with concern in his voice.

"Yes! Tell me!"

"A chair, some rope, a baseball bat and a lot of blood."

"That sick monster tortured my poor mother. I hate him!"

"I'm sorry, Nichelle," Renny said, reaching over and

stroking her hand.

"Continue."

"I was turning around about to leave and I noticed a purse in the corner and I figured it belonged to the now dead woman. I wanted to see the face of the person who Arnez felt the need to have bashed like that."

"Yeah, I can't wait for somebody to bash that nigga's face in!" Nichelle barked, getting extra amped.

Renny couldn't even say nothing in his cousin's defense because he knew he had that coming and deserved it, so instead he continued. "I had never seen your mother before but when I went through her wallet I saw a picture of a little girl and then a picture of you when you looked to be about fifteen or sixteen. Then I recognized the address on her driver's license. It was at that moment I knew the woman Arnez had killed was your mother. There was also a picture of a young teenage boy, and your mother holding a baby. On the back your mother wrote; Genesis, Genevieve my babies. And with the date on the back, I knew the baby had to be you and I figured Genesis must be your brother."

"Do you know my brother?" Renny could hear the hope in Nichelle's voice.

"No I don't. But I've heard Arnez speak of him on numerous occasions and it was never positive. That's his enemy. I knew Arnez was coming after you next but I didn't want him to know I was on to him so I sent Tierra to bring you to me."

"What happened to Tierra?"

"I was trying to call her and she wasn't answering her phone. I figured shit was fucked up but not that fucked up.

When I got to the projects, Arnez was gone and Tierra was laying on the sidewalk bleeding. I tried to save her but she was already dead."

Nichelle could no longer keep her composure. Tears gushed out her eyes and wouldn't stop. "I can't believe Tierra is dead," she screamed over and over again becoming inconsolable. Renny pulled over in an attempt to calm Nichelle down.

"Baby, it's gonna be alright. I'ma take care of you," he said pulling her close and wrapping his arms around Nichelle as her body continued to shake. "I promise, I'll make sure Arnez or nobody else ever harms you again."

Each Tear
Chapter 10

When Veronica woke up next to Arnez, two things crossed her mind: she couldn't believe she was going to be late for work but luckily she was the head of her own law firm and the sex had been incredible. But no matter how great the fuck, Veronica had work to do and clients that depended on her so she quietly began getting out of bed not wanting to awaken a sleeping Arnez.

"Where do you think you're going," Arnez said pulling Veronica back in bed.

"I thought you were asleep."

"Yeah, and tried to make an escape but you thought wrong. I'm not done with you yet," he said, pinning her down on the bed,

"Arnez, I have to go. I'm already late for work," she murmured in his ear trying not to enjoy the tongue play he was giving her body. But once the moistness of his mouth swallowed her hardened nipples her legs spread wide open as if he knocked on the front door and she personally invited him in.

"This dick feel good to you," Arnez more so stated than asked.

"Yeeessss," she moaned, briefly wondering how she went from both legs out the bed to full body back in the bed with her insides getting twisted out. While she wondered that, Arnez thought about how lucky he was to be swimming in some good pussy that would also help him finally get a firm grip on Nichelle once and for all.

"These pictures are incredible," T-Roc said to Akil as they went through some of the shots from Nichelle's photo shoot.

"Yeah, she's a natural."

"Akil, she's more than a natural. These pictures are phenomenal."

"What are you all in here going on and on about?" Genesis asked as he walked in T-Roc's office.

"I wasn't expecting to see you this early in the morning," T-Roc remarked.

"You told me to be here by ten. I'm taking my job very seriously."

"Akil, this is Genesis, my new go to man." They shook hands and then all three started looking at the photos. "This is the new spokes model for the perfume I was telling you about."

"She's beautiful," Genesis said, going through each picture.

"Don't get any ideas, no dating women that we work

with," T-Roc teased.

"Get the fuck outta here! She looks young enough to be my sister! That's your mind you need to get out the gutter," Genesis snapped back in a condescending way.

"But the thing is, she's not your sister so it's okay to lust just don't touch."

"Believe it or not, as pretty as she is I have absolutely no desire to lust or touch her. I don't know what it is but it would seem perverted to me for some reason, maybe because she has somewhat of an innocent thing going on."

"I don't see innocent. I see pure sexiness that's going to sell me a lot of perfume," T-Roc grinned.

"Genesis, I feel where you coming from and also feel where you coming from too, T-Roc. I think that's what makes Nichelle so appealing. She does have sex appeal but it almost appears harmless. That's why men and women will be drawn to her," Akil explained.

"So when will I have a chance to meet this Nichelle?"

"The next scheduled photo shoot is Friday, so be there."

"I will. I might need to protect her from certain married men," Genesis said eyeing T-Roc. It was all in fun but at the same time, Genesis knew you could never underestimate how far a man would go to get his hands on some fresh young meat. "So what's on today's agenda?"

"Let me wrap things up with Akil and then I wanted to go over a few things with you."

"Cool. I'ma step out and make a phone call. I'll be back shortly."

"So, Akil, how's Nichelle feeling about the shoot? I

thought she was going to come with you this morning to see the pictures."

"She was but she had to take care of some things."

"Really, is everything okay with her? I would hate for our rising star to be having problems already."

"No problems. Everything is good. Just minor kinks to work out but I'm on top of it."

"Yeah, make sure you do stay on top of it. I'm planning on investing a lot of money in her. I don't want anything to go wrong."

"It won't."

"I'ma take your word on that. But if you need my assistance in anyway, I'm here."

"Thanks."

"No need to thank me. We're doing business together. I have to protect my assets and Nichelle is now an asset. To show the industry and Nichelle just how invested I am in her, I'm throwing her a grand over-the-top, ridiculous coming out party," T-Roc boasted.

"Are you sure you want to do that?" Akil was surprised by T-Roc's suggestion.

"No, I'm not sure, I'm absolutely positive! I'm going all out. It'll be the biggest party of the year. I'm inviting all the industry bigwigs, entertainers, you name it. Not only will it give Nichelle a lot of exposure but I'll use it as a way to give my new perfume line great buzz. This is perfect!" Riding high off of his excitement, T-Roc picked up his desk phone and got his secretary on the phone. "I need you to call for a meeting ASAP! We have a party to plan."

When Precious woke up the only thing on her mind was the conversation she had with Quentin the day before. She never imagined it would have such a profound effect on her but it did. The idea of having a relationship with him was something she actually wanted to happen and it was somewhat scary to her.

"What has you in such deep thought?" Supreme questioned when he walked in the bedroom.

"Is it that obvious?" Precious wondered.

"Yeah, you're sitting up in bed, kinda in a daze, staring up. Either something is on your mind or you got a habit I don't know about," he taunted.

"Funny!" Precious took a pillow from off the bed and tossed it at Supreme. "No drug habit but I do have something on my mind."

"Care to share?"

"I do. It's about Quentin."

"Your father?"

"Wow, that's the first time you've ever called him that."

"Well, it's the first time you've ever mentioned him. Before it always seemed off limits, like we know who he is but don't say his name out loud."

"True."

"So what changed?"

"I had a long conversation with him yesterday and he isn't the loser I thought he was. I believe he actually loved my mother and in her own way she loved him too. But baby, you know how it is when you get caught up in the streets, things become different."

"I guess you're referring to your mother's drug habit?"

Precious put her head down and nodded. "That's still so hard for me. I lost so many years with my mother because of her addiction to drugs and now I find out that's the reason I lost growing up with my father too. But the one thing that gives me comfort is that I got to see my mother one last time before she died and she was clean."

A tear rolled down Precious' cheek as she flashed back to that day. Her mother looked so beautiful. She picked up weight and her hourglass shape was still intact. Her skin was glowing and her sandy brown hair was cut short and streaked with blond highlights. It made her green eyes stand out ever more. All the beauty that was hidden because of the drugs was now coming through. Precious hugged her mother so tightly and wouldn't let go. For the first time in her life she had a mother. Never did she think that would be the very last time she would see her alive.

"Baby, don't cry. Your mother is looking down on you, and trust me, she is so proud."

"You really think so?"

"I know so. And I think it's going to be good for you to have a relationship with your father, that's important. You owe it to yourself and him to at least try."

"I think so too. Plus, Aaliyah seems to really like him. I never knew either of my grandfathers, I think it's only right that Aaliyah have two," she smiled. "Speaking of Aaliyah, where is she, because it's awfully quiet?"

"I took her to my parent's house this morning. They wanted to take her to the zoo and keep her for a few days.

And I thought we could spend some quality time together. I want to take my beautiful wife out."

"You get no argument from me. So I guess that means we are going to be on the East Coast for a little while longer?"

"Yes. The business I'm handling is taking much longer than I anticipated but it has to be done."

"I understand and there is no place like NYC, so I'm good."

"I figured you would be. Now get over here and let's make a baby," Supreme said, pulling Precious into his arms ready to make love.

Renny sat on the chaise watching Nichelle sleep so peacefully. He had held her as she cried herself into a deep coma, one that she didn't seem to want to come out of. At least while she slept she wouldn't have to deal with the reality of her situation—that her life was in danger.

"Where am I?" Nichelle asked, still halfway asleep but trying to come out of her slumber.

"You're at my crib in Jersey. You don't remember coming here last night?"

"Sorta, but I was so upset I can't really remember much after you told me Tierra was dead. I still don't want to believe it."

"I know and I hate I had to tell you but you needed to know."

"I never wanted to be responsible for somebody dying. Even after what those girls did to me and Lerrick caused me to lose my baby, never did I wish her death. But what I feel for Arnez is beyond hate. I need him dead. Why won't you kill him, Renny?" Renny's eyes penetrated deeply into Nichelle's as if dissecting her soul. He knew from the intense glare she gave him back, Nichelle was serious with her request.

"Nichelle, life is much more complicated than that. I can't just kill Arnez."

"Oh really? You didn't seem to have a problem killing my man, one of my closest friends and two other men. So murdering four innocent people is all good but scum like Arnez is off limits. Maybe you were right, staying away from me was the best thing for both of us," Nichelle said before continuing to rip into Renny. "That motherfucker is responsible for killing not only Tierra but my mother and you want to talk about complicated. The only thing complicated is how the fuck did I ever let myself love you! You're just like him. You're nothing but a murderer too!"

Nichelle could see Renny's jaw line flinching. She remembered that would happen when he was ready to explode in anger, which wasn't often because he was the epitome of coolness. But Nichelle's own anger wouldn't allow her to let up. She kept to the tongue lashing until as swift as lightening flashing Renny got a hold of Nichelle and clenched her arms so tightly, it felt like her blood circulation had been cut off.

"Stop talking before you make me snap your neck," Renny stated, without even slightly raising his voice. "If it wasn't for me, you would be dead. Up until recently, each man that Arnez hired to snatch you up worked for me. So

I was able to make sure it never happened. This last cat Arnez hired isn't on my payroll. That's why I reached out to you because I could no longer protect you from a distance. But best believe all I've done, is to guarantee you stay alive."

"Everything but kill the person who is responsible for this madness!"

"Killing Arnez ain't the right move yet. It has to be executed properly. Besides us doing business together, he is my blood. But this obsession he has with taking down that dude Genesis is fucking his head up on so many levels. Trust me; I'm working on permanently getting rid of Arnez once and for all."

"First of all, Genesis isn't some dude, he's my brother. And I want him alive. He's all the family I have left." Renny let go of Nichelle's arms and shook his head, clearly frustrated.

"I'm doing everything to keep you alive, now you telling me to worry about keeping somebody I don't even know alive too. Nichelle, I understand you want to find your brother but I don't know what more I can do."

"Help me find my brother. He needs to know that Arnez is out to destroy him and trying to use me to do it."

"Nichelle, this isn't some random beef. Your brother and my cousin were both in love with the same woman. Genesis is well aware he is on Arnez's hit list as I'm sure my cousin is on his list too."

"My mother dying and my best friend are all over a woman?"

"Yes. Remember when we had dinner at Arnez's house and you commented on the woman in the picture?"

"Of course, I couldn't believe how much she looked like my mother."

"That's her, Talisa."

"Talisa," Nichelle repeated her name as if it helped her to process everything Renny had told her. "So which one of them is she with?"

"Neither, she's dead."

"What! She's dead too. This is crazy! You seem to know a lot about my brother's life, so where is he?"

"Nichelle, I don't know. This information is all from casual conversation with Arnez. I can't dig too deep because I don't want him to get suspicious. He don't have a clue that I know you and Genesis are related. He left Tierra dead and he knew we broke up and I told him we haven't had any contact. So asking questions about you and your brother would only raise red flags."

"So how long am I going to have to watch my back?"

"Hopefully not that much longer. Like I said, I'm working on it. It's good you have that bodyguard and I have some people keeping a watchful eye on you too. We just have to be extra cautious."

Nichelle sat down on the bed as if defeated. A lot of her questions had been answered but now a whole slew of other issues presented themselves and she had no idea how to resolve them. But with all the disarray Nichelle was more determined than ever to find Genesis. The more Renny told her, the closer she felt to her brother and that sooner or later they would cross paths.

"Precious, thank you for coming," Quentin said, standing up and pulling out her seat. When Quentin invited Precious for lunch he wasn't sure she would accept and it turned out to be a pleasant surprise when she did.

"When I told you I wanted to try and have a relationship with you, I meant it."

"Showing up today has made me a believer and again, I thank you."

"Would you stop, you sound like I'm doing you a favor or something."

"Maybe because that's how I feel."

"Are you ready to order?" The waiter asked, catching them off guard. Quentin and Precious had quickly become engaged in what each other had to say. Food was now an afterthought.

"I need a few more minutes but you can bring me some water with lemon."

"And you, sir?"

"The same but no lemon." Quentin then turned his attention back to his daughter. "Like I was saying, part of me does feel like you're doing me a favor."

"Why is that?"

"Because you're allowing me to connect with you and make up for all the time we lost. That's healing to me. You could've very well turned your back on me and not allowed me that opportunity."

"Well then you're doing me a favor too because deep down inside I always wanted a father. I tried to pretend that I didn't care either way but I was lying to myself."

"I think this will be a healing process for both of us."

"I hope so, because as I get older I'm realizing more and more that healing is good for the soul."

Quentin smiled at Precious feeling as if they were already beginning to make inroads "That makes me so proud to hear, Precious. It's wonderful to know you're at that place in your life because there is one other person you need to begin the healing process with."

"Who would that be?" Precious inquired, completely baffled as to who he could be speaking of.

"Your sister—Maya."

"That heffa is not my sister!"

"Precious, keep your voice down," Quentin recommended, noticing several patrons turn their head in their direction because of how loud and bold Precious voice was, when making her statement.

"Don't tell me to keep my voice down! I'll be damned if I'm going to talk low when it comes to that menace."

"Weren't you just speaking about being in a different place in your life and healing being good for the soul? I know your feelings couldn't have changed in less than thirty seconds."

"When it comes to Maya my feelings will never change. That chick is a bad seed...point blank. She not even worth any airtime. Maya is lucky to be alive because I was this close to killing her ass," Precious made clear, making a small space between her thumb and index finger.

"Deep down there is a reason you didn't kill Maya. And it's because you didn't want to have the blood of your sister on your hands."

"No, it's because I didn't want to rot in jail behind

fuckin' up that triflin' ho! I had a daughter to raise and a husband to go home to. I wasn't about to throw all that away to get momentary pleasure out of killing Maya. That's why I didn't slit that heffa's throat...end of story. So don't turn this into some long lost sister's reunite."

"That's not what I'm trying to do."

"That's what it sounds like to me."

"The fact is, whether you want to accept it or not, Maya is your sister. You need to get some sort of closure."

"I got all the closure I needed when she was found guilty and they sent her psycho ass to jail."

Quentin shook his head in frustration. "All I'm asking is you have a conversation with Maya."

"A conversation about what? Why she fucked my husband? Why she orchestrated the kidnapping of my child and *your* granddaughter? Oh, and let's not forget, why she left me for dead after kidnapping me too and making my husband believe I left him to be with Nico. Is that the conversation you want me to have with that crazy bat because if so I'll pass."

"I'm not excusing Maya's actions but a lot of what she did was because she was being manipulated by Mike."

"Is that the line she's running with...let me blame it on my dead brother who can't defend himself. Mike was no saint and if I hadn't witnessed the mayhem first hand I might even fall for that bullshit Maya is feeding you. But see I was there, and I know who the ringleader was and it wasn't Mike, it was Maya."

"Precious, I know those are the facts as you see them and I'm not going to try and change your mind."

"Wise decision."

"But both of you are my daughters and I missed out on being a part of your lives. I feel a lot of responsibility in how Maya turned out, because unlike you I did know she was my daughter and I should've played an active role in her life. Maybe if I had, she wouldn't be in the predicament she is in now."

"Wow, that scheming ass heffa has really done a number on you," Precious said, shaking her head.

"Precious, please, just listen."

"I'm listening," Precious said, as she simultaneously rolled her eyes and turned her head away.

"You won't understand the burden I'm carrying until you watch your own daughter grow up and deal with her issues."

"Are you comparing Aaliyah to Maya?"

"No, what I'm saying is, as a parent you feel responsible, whether good or bad, for the impact your child makes in their life. Maya has clearly made a very bad impact and as her father I feel a great deal of responsibility. We both pray that you never have to deal with major hardships with Aaliyah, but as a parent you never know what you'll endure. The only thing that's for certain is that you'll never give up on your child so I have to be there for Maya."

"Yeah, maybe so but I don't. She's your daughter, not mine."

"But you're my daughter and I'm asking as your father, to please go visit Maya in jail. Just have one conversation with your sister."

"Is it really that important to you?"

"Yes, it is. I don't believe either one of you will truly be able to move forward in your life if you don't do this."

"Quentin, you have to promise me that if I do what you ask, and go see Maya you will never ask me to do it again. This will be the one and only time."

"I promise but I ask you go see her with an open mind and open heart. After you all talk if you still have no desire to start fresh and begin building a relationship with your sister I won't pressure you to do so."

"Fine, I'll go see Maya. But remember the promise you made me because after I see her, I'm done."

Chapter 11

For the next week, Arnez spent all his time wining, dining and fucking Veronica. With the constant pipe he was laying, she had become completely dick whipped. Then for an added bonus Arnez showered her with pricey gifts, which made Veronica believe she had found the perfect man. She wasn't comprehending it was all a set up in order for him to get complete control over her mind, which she seemed more than willing to let happen.

"You're the kind of man I've been waiting for my entire life," Veronica revealed as she laid up with Arnez on a dreary Saturday afternoon. With the sound of the rain pouring down and the warmth of Arnez's strong arms wrapped around her naked body, it gave Veronica the false impression that they were a legitimate couple. She basked in the phony romantic aura Arnez had tossed on her.

"And you're the type of woman I've always dreamed of making my wife." Veronica's ears perked up and both eyebrows rose. That was the last thing she expected for

Arnez to say. She had dallied with her fair share of street dudes and none of them had ever mentioned making her their wife, even the relationships that lasted for an extended period of time. She always assumed that none of them wanted to get tied down to a career woman like her. They like to play but after awhile they grew bored and it was on to the next one.

"Do you mean that?" Veronica asked without looking up. Deep down she didn't want to make eye contact, in case he was lying and the evidence was written on his face.

"Of course, or I wouldn't have said it," Arnez replied as he gently stroked the side of Veronica's arm. "I never believed it was possible to find a woman with all the qualities I desired until meeting you." Arnez words were sweet music to Veronica's ears. How sincere and genuine Arnez sounded gave Veronica the confidence to make the eye contact she was initially avoiding.

"Thank you for saying that, you have no idea how much that means to me." And it did mean a lot to Veronica. She had been in a relationship with another man for the last year that seemed to be going nowhere. He had the prerequisites that she was drawn to in a lover: emotionally detached, married to the game of illegal activities and great in bed. Veronica thought she had played her cards perfectly with him, but he never wanted to take it to the next level. He seemed more interested in picking her brilliant brain for legal information than making a love connection. It was to the point that Veronica no longer felt their relationship was an even exchange. It was like she was simply being used at his convenience. But the sex was great, although it had almost become obsolete. Before she was willing to take what she could get because her attraction to him was so powerful. But now that Arnez was on the scene the tides had changed.

"Does that mean you would one day consider being my wife?"

"Are you proposing to me?" Veronica couldn't contain the smile that had taken over her face.

"I guess you can say that. I know that I want to marry you, but before I go any further I want to know that you would want to marry me too. You know I can be sensitive and I don't want you to bruise my ego too much," he grinned.

"You don't have to worry about that. Because when you do decide to pop the question, you will no doubt get a big yes from me."

"That's all I needed to hear," Arnez said, before locking lips with Veronica and giving her another dick down that was slowly turning her mind to mush.

"So you're going to stand there with a blank stare on your face and not answer my question?" By the tone of Akil's question it was evident he was losing his patience with Nichelle. His boyish looking face seemed to be aging in less than sixty seconds. And his slender build wasn't appearing to be so nonthreatening anymore. Nichelle knew she had to proceed with caution and choose her words wisely.

"Akil, I apologize for not getting in touch with you sooner but I needed a break."

"A break! You call disappearing for two days a break!" Akil yelled. He had never raised his voice to Nichelle and it was starting to freak her out.

"Calm down. You're getting upset for nothing," she said coolly, trying to downplay the severity of the situation. "It wasn't a full two days, it was more like a day and a half."

"This is bullshit, Nichelle. I want to know what the hell is going on with you."

"I told you, I needed time to myself. Everything is moving so fast."

"Everything like what?"

"This modeling career."

"I thought this is what you wanted?"

"I do but…"

"But what? Tell me what is going on. I can't help you if I don't know what is causing you to act like this."

"That's the thing. I don't want your help."

"Excuse me?" From the irritated expression on Akil's face, Nichelle knew her choice of words were wrong.

"What I'm trying to say is that only time is going to make this better, not you helping me. Do you understand?"

"No I don't. I believe you're bullshitting me and I don't like it."

"I don't know what to say."

"How about starting with the truth. Who were you with?"

"I was by myself."

"Where did you go?"

"I told you already, I stayed in a hotel?"

"How did you get there?"

"I took a taxi…enough of this interrogation! I fucked

up. I shouldn't have disappeared, but I asked you for time alone and you wouldn't give it to me so I took it. Are you satisfied," Nichelle belted. She walked towards the huge window and stared outside. The view of Central Park gave her a serene feeling that had been lacking in what felt like forever. "I don' think I can do this anymore."

"I don't want to fight about this anymore either. You answered my questions and I'll leave it at that."

"I'm not talking about us arguing."

"Then what are you talking about?"

"This modeling career. I don't think I can do it anymore. It's just too much."

"What! You're about to have your big breakthrough, what are you talking about?"

"Maybe I'm not ready for a big breakthrough or maybe I don't want it. This life in front of a camera, I don't think it's for me. I'm not cut out for it."

"Wait, back up. Where is all this coming from?"

"This argument got me thinking and this may not be the right path for me."

"Nichelle, I pushed too hard and I apologize. I was worried about you. It was only a few weeks ago that a man tried to snatch you up in the middle of the street. I worry about you."

"I understand but having my face plastered everywhere might make things worse."

"That's why you have security, so you can be protected."

"But I don't want to live my life like that, walking around with security. I want to be free to do what I want to do."

"Which is what?"

"I don't know, maybe go to college or get married and be a wife and mother. All I know is that I want some peace in my life."

"You're living in this beautiful loft overlooking Central Park and you talk about wanting peace in your life. How much more peaceful can things be for you."

"This isn't the life I want."

"Fine, Nichelle. I'm not going to try and change your mind. I think you're a natural but if this isn't the career you want then so be it. After you finish this perfume campaign I won't get you any new work."

"I don't want to finish the perfume campaign. It's still early, I'm sure T-Roc can find another girl."

"You signed a contract."

"I know, but I haven't spent any of the money yet. I'll give it back."

"Okay, Nichelle, you're talking crazy. You can't do this. Business isn't conducted in this manner. You have an obligation to fulfill."

"I have other obligations I need to focus on right now."

"Other obligations like what? What can be so important that you have to throw everything we've been building away? Not only that but think about T-Roc and what he's invested. He's already planning this huge party for you that's happening in less than two weeks. You may not care about your career but what about my reputation. While you're running off trying to find peace, I still have to do business with these people. So instead of just thinking about yourself put me in the equation too."

"Fine! I'll finish this perfume campaign but after this I'm focusing on what's important to me." For Nichelle, that was finding her brother Genesis. After everything Renny revealed to her, that was her number one priority. He was all the family she had. Nichelle felt that with all the time it required to have a successful modeling career, she rather put that energy towards uniting with her brother. Of course Nichelle wasn't willing to share that with Akil because then she would have to open the door and reveal all her skeletons. But after her gig was up she would walk away and not look back. Her focus would be on finding Genesis.

Genesis woke up surrounded by the warm walls of CoCo and it felt like home—comfortable and content. Their relationship easily transitioned from friends to lovers without any major collisions. Mainly because CoCo had studied the dos and don'ts of Genesis so thoroughly she was able to play her position to perfection.

One rule that was easy for CoCo to follow was Genesis' love for morning sex. With each thrust, CoCo wrapped her thick thighs tighter around Genesis' back so his tool could go deeper inside. His hands rested firmly on her ample ass, lifting it up, letting his dick get lost in her juices. "If I had known you would feel this good, I would've never waited this long," Genesis said, between strokes.

"That's okay, as long as you never make me wait again." The seductive tone in CoCo's voice made Genesis swim even deeper, hitting every spot. After each stroke CoCo began clenching her moist lips down on Genesis' manhood causing him to reach an escalated eruption.

"Oh shiiiit," they both echoed simultaneously, reaching their climax.

"You're incredible," Genesis finally said, after catching his breath.

"So are you."

"Never did I think it could be this right between us. Friendship, business and great sex, it's almost too perfect."

"No, it just means we're right for each other but I always knew that."

"Did you now?"

"Yes, but I've been waiting for you to realize that."

"What if I told you I have?"

"I would say, don't play with me, Genesis, because you know I'm in love with you."

"That's one thing I promise you, no games. I respect you and our friendship way too much for that. My feelings for you are real and I want to see how far we can go with this."

"Are you talking about the possibility of a serious relationship?"

"Yes, that's exactly what I'm talking about. At first I wasn't sure that could be possible between us but I was wrong. You've shown me that maybe we can have it all."

"Genesis, if you do decide to let our relationship go in that direction, I'll do everything in my power to make sure it's one decision you'll never regret."

"I believe you and that makes me want to step my game up and please you and make you happy."

"Being with you does make me happy," CoCo smiled and her entire face lit up. At that moment, Genesis saw CoCo in an entirely different light. She appeared sweet and vulnerable as if he needed to protect her. There was no edge or toughness only a look of pure and honest love.

"Listen, there's a big party coming up that T-Roc is throwing for the model of his new perfume line. I want you to come, not as one of my business partners, or a friend but as my date."

"Are you sure?"

"You know me well enough that I don't say or do anything unless I'm sure."

"Genesis Taylor, I'm going to make you so happy, you'll never want to leave me."

"No sense in waiting, let's start right now," Genesis said before entering back inside of CoCo.

When Veronica got back home after spending the weekend with Arnez, the first thing she wanted to do was take a long hot bath. Arnez had worn her body out. His sex drive was off the charts and keeping up with him was proving to be harder work than any legal case she had ever taken on.

Veronica dropped her keys on the stand right next to the door when you entered her apartment. Before going to her bedroom, her heels clicked on the bamboo flooring as she made a quick stop in the kitchen. She glanced at the European styled cabinetry before retrieving a crystal glass and bottle of Merlot.

Veronica then went in the living room and closed the custom-made drapes on the floor-to-ceilings windows before heading to the bedroom. She slipped out of the silk wrap dress and four-inch heels she was wearing and went into the master bathroom. Her eyes darted to the shower area as the mosaic marble mural surrounded by honed marble tile for the walls, ceiling and seat was calling her name but her body needed the whirlpool tucked into a bay window. Veronica turned on the water trying to make sure she got the perfect percentage mix of hot and cold before adding her combination of bubble bath and oils.

"This is exactly what I need," Veronica said out loud turning on a CD of soothing music and sipping on her wine. When she stepped in the tub the hot water penetrated every muscle in her body, sending a relaxing tingle up her spine.

"Where have you been?" The question from the familiar male voice made Veronica's eyes open wide.

"Delondo, what are you doing here?"

"I've been calling you all weekend and I couldn't get in touch with you. I was concerned and I missed you. What had you so occupied this weekend?"

"I had to attend a business conference. I got back tonight?"

"You weren't allowed phone calls?"

"Funny…the hotel I was staying at had horrible phone reception."

"I see," Delondo muttered as if he only somewhat believed Veronica's excuse.

"So you came all the way from Philly because you

couldn't get in touch with me? That's interesting since I haven't been able to get you on the phone in over a week."

"I've been busy. But I have some business I need to handle in New York and I need your assistance on some legal issues I have questions about."

"I should've known," Veronica groaned, rolling her eyes. "Being concerned and missing me was nothing but a bunch of crock. I'm surprised you kept a hold of the key I gave you since you probably never had any intentions of ever using it."

"You're in rare form tonight. That trip must've stressed you out."

"No, you're the stress. I'm tired of you taking me for granted and popping up when you feel like it. We've been seeing each other for almost a year now but yet you make me feel like I'm an afterthought to you."

Delondo calmly nodded his head, soaking up what Veronica was saying. "So what, you're gettin' some new dick and feeling yourself now, is that it?"

"Fuck you, Delondo!" she yelled and then tossed a wet soap sponge at him, hitting his right shoulder.

"Is that a yes or no?" Delondo's calm and somewhat nonchalant attitude was infuriating Veronica even more.

"It's not like you care either way."

"Just answer the question. If you're seeing somebody else I'll give you your key back and I won't bother you anymore."

"No, I'm not seeing anybody else," she lied. As much as Veronica hated the way Delondo treated her she wasn't ready to let him go. Even with Arnez in the picture, twisting her back out on the regular, Veronica had to prove to herself that she could make Delondo want to be with her.

"Then stop with the extra drama and just be happy to see me. The drive made me tired. I'ma go lay down." When Delondo walked out the bathroom all Veronica could do was shake her head. He had given her the perfect opportunity for an exit but she didn't take it. Instead, she would have to get her energy up and fuck the shit out of him so he wouldn't know the next man had worn her out.

"Thank goodness I did take this bath," Veronica mumbled under her breath before closing her eyes. She wanted to soak it up for a few more minutes before going to put her work in.

"When our father said you were coming to see me, I didn't believe him. But here you are."

"Pathological liars usually do have a hard time believing that people can tell the truth."

"All I was trying to say is that I'm glad you came. I know it must've been difficult for you."

"Yes, it was difficult but I'm here."

"Did you tell Supreme you were coming?"

"Why, were you hoping he would join me for this visitation?" Precious questioned with dry sarcasm. "It's a shame. You're still not over your sick obsession with him."

"I don't know what you're talking about."

"I can see it in your eyes, Maya." Precious leaned in closer before continuing, "Perpetrate all you like but you can't mask the craziness from me."

"This isn't about Supreme. I wanted to connect with you, we are sisters."

"By DNA only!"

"Precious, why did you come if you have no interest in at least making an attempt to start over and build a relationship?"

"Because Quentin asked me to, that's the only reason."

"But you're not even trying."

"Maya, I don't care what sort of bullshit story you fed Quentin I know you're a psycho. To pretend otherwise would be a joke."

"I'm not going to hit you with excuses for some of the things I did but you have to believe that I want to make amends with you. I've always admired you and even before I found out we were blood related I loved you like a sister."

"That's why you left me for dead and threatened to hurt my daughter if I didn't cooperate with you." Maya put her head down not addressing what Precious said. "Oh, you don't want to speak on that. Either you want to make amends or you don't."

"Of course I do."

"Then you need to admit what you did to me and stop trying to pull the wool over Quentin's eyes."

"I admit I made some mistakes but not everything happened the way that it seems."

"I get it. That's the story you're running with for appeal purposes. Good luck with that because it won't work!"

"How can you hate me so much but yet you were able to forgive Nico and welcome him back into your bed after he shot you?"

"Listen, you delusional, bitch. What happened between me and Nico has nothing to do with what you did, there is no comparison. You're a fuckin' nut who needs to stay exactly where you are—behind bars."

"I'm really sorry you feel that way, Precious. I was hoping we could come to some sort of understanding. But it's clear you have no intentions of letting that happen. But there is no way I'm spending the rest of my life locked away like some animal."

"But that's what you are and what you deserve."

"Then I need to toss you some prison attire because you should be right here with me. Have you forgotten all the blood you have on your hands?"

Precious stared at Maya. Her hair was pulled back in a French braid. It was the first time she had studied her face since finding out they were related. Features that she had previously brushed off as being similar now had reason behind them. The full pouty lips they both had, the shape of their eyes and distinctive bone structure, all inherited from Quentin. As much as Precious wanted to, there was no denying the resemblance. Then there was the slick ass mouth Maya had. Precious wasn't sure if that was their shared genetics or just some slum street shit.

"Listen, stop with all the comparison shit. It doesn't matter where you think I should be. The point is, you're behind bars and I'm not."

"You still only give a fuck about yourself. You might *think* I'm psycho but I know for a fact that only ice runs through your veins."

"You're right. You get no argument from me there."

"Your feelings towards me really haven't changed the least, even though you know we're sisters."

"Yeah, I actually find you more repulsive, which I thought was impossible. See, because of that unfortunate error it makes me unable to kill you. So I guess I'm not as cold as we both thought."

Maya shook her head in dismay before saying, "One day you *will* need me and the funny part is, I'ma come through for you. We'll see how repulsive I am to you then, my dear sister. Now excuse me, this visitation is over," were Maya's parting words as she walked away leaving Precious slightly puzzled.

Love Is My Disease
Chapter 12

Nichelle was about to step in the shower when she heard her iPhone beep, letting her know she received a text message.

Meet me @ my place ASAP. Emergency!

Renny

"I wonder what's wrong?" she questioned out loud. But instead of bombarding Renny with questions, Nichelle simply sent a text back letting him know she was on the way. Instead of taking the long, hot shower she had been looking forward to, Nichelle stuck to the basics and was in and out.

After pulling her hair in a ponytail and throwing on some sweats with a t-shirt, she grabbed her purse and was out.

As the taxi pulled up to Renny's townhouse in Jersey, Nichelle was all sorts of anxious. He hadn't sent any additional text messages and neither did she. All Nichelle wanted to do was get face to face with him and find out what was so urgent. She figured it pertained to Arnez but hoped that Renny had found the whereabouts to her brother.

Nichelle rung the doorbell a couple of times and let out a long huff when Renny didn't answer. "I know he didn't bounce," she said looking at her watch. It didn't even take me that long to get here," she continued talking out loud as she knocked on the door. When the door finally opened, Nichelle stepped back and reached for the stair banister, as she was about to fall.

"Nichelle, it's okay. Here, take my hand so you don't fall." At first Nichelle resisted. She was completely freaked out. But as the initial shock waned, she was able to do so. "Can I get you something to drink?"

"No, I just need to sit down."

"Come on; let's go in the living room." Nichelle followed still not fully comprehending what her eyes were seeing. "I know you're surprised to see me."

"Yeah, especially since Renny told me you were dead."

"That's what he told you?" Tierra asked, somewhat dumbfounded.

"Yes, he did." Nichelle stood and looked at Tierra for a brief moment as if taking in the fact that what she was seeing in front of her eyes was real. "Oh, Tierra, I'm so happy you're alive," Nichelle finally said and hugged her best friend tightly. "I was so worried about you."

"I worried everyday about you. It was killing me to

stay away from you but with all the craziness going on it was for the best."

"So what happened? Where have you been and why did Renny tell me you were dead?"

"Girl, where do I start? How 'bout wit' that fool ass nigga Arnez. Him and that ruthless Chanel really left me on the sidewalk for dead. If Renny hadn't showed up I would've bleed to death right there in the Queens projects."

"So Renny saved your life?"

"Yep. After he took me to the hospital, I was there for a few weeks. Then when they was ready to release me he stashed me at one of his other cribs in Jersey so Arnez couldn't find me. He didn't want Arnez to know I was still alive."

"Why, because he was afraid that Arnez would try to finish you off?"

"That, and if Arnez knew Renny saved me then he would also know Renny knew about what he did to your mother and that he was trying to get you. Renny wanted Arnez to think he was in the dark about all that while he plotted to make his move."

"So Renny was telling me the truth when he said he wanted to get rid of Arnez?"

"Definitely! I mean that is his cousin and they do a lot of business together but Renny mos def want Arnez out the picture. He just tryna figure out how and the right time to make it happen."

"So you've being keeping a low profile all this time?"

"Yeah, and the shit has been driving me crazy. I've only seen my mom a few times. But she understand I'm damn near under the witness protection program right now," Tierra joked.

"But why did Renny want me to believe you were dead? I wouldn't have told anybody what was going on."

"I know. I was a tad stunned when you told me that," Tierra explained shrugging her arms. "But he didn't even want me to know he had made contact with you."

"What do you mean?"

"I knew he always had some people watching out for you. You know to make sure Arnez was never able to snatch you up. But when I would ask about you, he always said, he hadn't spoken to you."

"That was true. The first time I actually heard from him was a few weeks ago."

"Yeah, he told me after I saw your bracelet. At first he denied it but I knew it was yours. It was the canary and white diamond bracelet Carmelo gave you for your birthday. I never saw nobody else with a bracelet like that."

"I left it over here the other day. Renny said he would give it to me next time I saw him. Is it here?"

"No, I think Renny has it with him."

"I thought he would be here, he sent me a text."

"Actually I sent you the text from his phone. Of course he don't know that," Tierra smirked. "When he told me he talked to you, I went through his phone while he was in the shower. When I sent you the text I was happy you hit me right back because of course I had to delete both of them."

"I see you still slick as hell! You better be lucky, I didn't call him or text again before I got here."

"Who you telling! Renny would have a fit if he knew

we were talking right now."

"Maybe, but he had to know that eventually he would have to come clean. I mean he can't pretend that you're dead forever."

"True. Because as soon as this shit is handled with Arnez I'm breaking free. I feel like a prisoner."

"I know what you mean!"

"Yeah, but at least you able to be out and about. I want to go shopping and rock some fly shit!"

"You will, but you maintaining. You still look official. I see you put on a little weight but it look good on you."

"Yep, I did but that's because…" right before Tierra could finish her sentence Nichelle heard what sounded like crying. She looked around to see where the noise was coming from and noticed a baby monitor.

"There's a baby here?"

"Hun huh, I'll be right back," Tierra said and disappeared upstairs. When she came back a few minutes later she was holding what looked to be a newborn.

"Is that your baby?" Nichelle's question was filled with astonishment.

"Yes, his name is Elijah."

"That's Renny's middle name. Wait, please don't tell me that's Renny's baby." Nichelle started backing away, shaking her head in complete confusion.

"I didn't want you to find out this way. But when Elijah woke up I really couldn't keep the secret anymore."

"So all that time when you and Renny were keeping secrets from me about what happened to Carmelo you were also having sex the entire time!"

"No! I swear, Nichelle. We didn't become intimate until after I got shot. After I started staying at his crib and I got better, one day it just happened."

Nichelle slumped down on the sofa as if defeated. "You've been playing house with my boyfriend and now you all have a baby together and you want to say one day it just happened. Wow, only you Tierra. Only you can say some bullshit like that with a straight face."

"Technically, Nichelle, he wasn't your boyfriend."

"But you knew I was still in love with him."

"No I didn't. When you found out that he was responsible for Carmelo's death you left that hotel room saying you wanted nothing else to do with him."

"So of course being the hoochie you are, you felt it was open season to get at my man, because whether we were together or not he was still my man and should've been off limits to you!"

"Nichelle, I was alone and stuck in the house. Renny was the only man available to me. I'm not trying to excuse what I did but my circumstances left me with little to no options."

"A baby," Nichelle said trying to contain her sniffles. "I lost a baby by a man I loved and now you have a baby by a man I'm in love with. How fuckin' unlucky am I."

"Nichelle, I'm so sorry," Tierra said sitting down next to her on the couch holding Elijah. As beautiful as the baby was, it was breaking Nichelle's heart to be next to him.

"I can't do this," Nichelle admitted, standing up from the couch and grabbing her purse.

"You're leaving?"

"Yes. I found my best friend and lost her again all in the same day."

"Nichelle, don't say that. We can get past this like we have everything else."

Right when Nichelle was about to respond both ladies turned their heads as they heard the front door opening. Renny came inside, noticed both women and calmly closed the door. When he walked up to them, with unruffled composure he took his son out of Tierra's hands and cradled him in his strong arms.

Nichelle kept the silence going and kept to her original plan which was to leave.

"Where are you going?" Renny directed his question to Nichelle with such ease as if she hadn't just found out he made a baby with her best friend.

"I'm going home."

"I'll take you," he responded, handing Elijah back over to Tierra.

"That's okay. You need to stay here and be with your baby."

"I said I would take you home." Renny reached out and grabbed Nichelle's arm, freezing her movement.

"Let go of me!" She belted trying to free her arm but his grasp was too firm. Renny gave Nichelle a glare that sent a shiver through her body. After all this time his hold over her was as powerful as ever.

"Come sit down." Renny gently released Nichelle's arm and guided her back over to the couch. "I see Tierra took it upon herself to get you over here and tell you about our baby," he said not once looking in Tierra's direction.

"Why didn't you tell me, or were you just going to continue making me believe that Tierra was dead?"

"I was going to tell you everything at the right time."

"When was the right time gonna be? I'm almost numb to you at this fuckin' point, Renny!"

"You know I hate when you raise your voice at me."

"And I hate that you put your dick in my best friend's pussy, how about that."

"It only happened a couple of times."

"And I'm supposed to believe that."

"Tierra, tell Nichelle how many times we had sex."

"Like twice," Tierra answered putting her head down.

"It doesn't matter; it was enough for you all to make a baby together. And the more I think about it you two are a much better fit than we ever was. You're completely ruthless and Tierra is the definition of trifling—a perfect match."

"Tierra, take Elijah upstairs."

"I need to set some things straight with Nichelle before I go anywhere," Tierra popped.

"What did I say?" Tierra rolled her eyes and then did as Renny directed.

"I understand you're upset. I made a mistake one that I regret but that doesn't change my feelings for you."

"It amazes me how you're able to switch shit up like it isn't a big deal. You have a baby with my best friend, everything has changed!"

"Are you saying because of the baby I have with Tierra, you're no longer in love with me?"

"What I'm saying is that I should've been done with

you when I found out all the fucked up shit you did. But if that wasn't enough to make me stay away from you, this surly is. I'm done for good this time and my only regret is wasting this past year wishing we were back together."

"I can't let you leave me."

"You don't have a choice. I don't care what I have to do but I will get you out of my system once and for all because you're poison."

Veronica was looking forward to having dinner with Arnez. She hadn't been able to see him the last few days due to Delondo's unexpected visit. When he had to abruptly cut his trip short due to a business emergency that was taking him to Memphis, the first thing Veronica did was call Arnez.

"Baby, I missed you," Arnez said, giving Veronica a kiss on the lips when she arrived.

"I missed you more," she smiled. "Thank you for meeting me for dinner at such short notice."

"Of course. I was surprised you called since you said you would be out of town for the next few days."

"My trip was cut short and you were the first person I wanted to see when I got back."

"That's perfectly fine with me because like I said, I missed you. I didn't realize how much until seeing you again." Veronica couldn't stop herself from blushing as she took in Arnez's bullshit.

"What are you doing next Wednesday?"

"Wednesday...I think I'm supposed to be going out of town. If I'm not mistaken I have to go to Atlanta and handle some business."

"That's too bad. I wanted you to attend this launch party for one of my clients with me."

"Launch party, for what client?" Arnez asked, trying not to sound too interested although he was.

"Oh, a young lady who is doing a campaign for a new perfume line. The party should be nice. T-Roc is giving it and his extravagance is legendary in the industry."

"Hate that I have to miss it. Where is this extravagant party going to take place?"

"The Plaza Hotel in the Grand Ballroom, like I said T-Roc is going all out. It's actually very smart marketing. He's using it as a tool to introduce Nichelle and get buzz and a ton of press for his new perfume line. I apologize; I'm talking about these people as if you know them. I'm sure you've heard of the multi-media mogul T-Roc and Nichelle is the client I was telling you about."

"I see. The Plaza, that's over there on Fifth Avenue and Central Park South—right?"

"The one and only."

"That should be quite a party. I wish I could be there."

"Me too. I'm ready to show you off."

"We have plenty of time for that. I'm not going anywhere," he said reaching across the table and stroking Veronica's hand. Arnez felt that sniffing up under Veronica's ass for all these weeks had finally paid off. With the information she revealed, Veronica had basically handed Nichelle over to Arnez on a silver platter. He would no doubt use it to his full advantage and as he held Veronica's hand the plotting began.

So Ambitious

Chapter 13

"Nichelle, you have to stop disappearing like this…it's getting ridiculous!"

"Akil, I told you an emergency came up the other day. But it's been handled."

"What's going to be your excuse next time, because there always seems to be one."

"No more excuses. I guarantee you there will be no more disappearing acts."

"How can you be so sure?"

"I just am." Right at that moment, Nichelle's cell began ringing and she saw it was Renny calling for the hundredth time. Ever since she left his townhouse a few days ago he had been blowing up her phone. Renny either didn't want to believe or couldn't believe that when Nichelle said she was done, she meant it.

"Are you going to answer that?" Akil questioned since this was at least the fourth or fifth time her phone had rung during their conversation but yet Nichelle ignored the call.

"No, and as a matter of fact I need to change my number."

"Why, is somebody harassing you? I can put a trace on the call."

"It's not that, I'm just ready for a fresh start. You know a clean slate. I think a new number is a good start."

Akil raised an eyebrow, showing his suspicion about the reason Nichelle was giving but he didn't take it any further. "Then it's done. You can toss that phone. I'll get you a new phone and number through my company, so you don't even have to worry about getting a bill."

"Works for me."

"Now that we've gotten that minor issue squared away, on to more important things, like are you ready for your party on Wednesday?"

"I can't believe it's here already, time is literally flying."

"I know but that's a good thing. That means you're a busy girl, making major moves."

"From what I hear T-Roc is pulling out all the stops for this event."

"That's what I hear too. He hired that event planner Bronson Van Wyck and he only handles big dog shit. But this is going to be great publicity for you. Although you probably don't care since you're taking an extended break from modeling once you're finished with this campaign."

"I'm not so sure about that anymore. Maybe it wouldn't be such a bad idea for me to give this whole career thing my all. I mean you only live once."

"What's with this change of attitude? Last time we spoke you wanted to focus on other things and leave this modeling shit alone."

"I do have something very important that I want to focus on but I think I can do both, especially since I put closure to an issue that was a heavy burden on me."

"That's good to hear because I believe the sky's the limit for you, Nichelle. You have something special, I see it, T-Roc clearly sees it or he wouldn't be investing all this money in you. The only person who needs to believe it now is you."

"I'm working on it, trust me."

"That's all I ask. Now I have to go, there's a meeting I have to attend. But don't forget you have a fitting at four o'clock."

"That's right! I've had so much on my mind, I almost forgot."

"You can't afford to forget. Wednesday will be your night to shine so your outfit can't be nothing short of perfection. But from what I understand your stylist has nothing but fiyah lined up."

"Well, I'll be there." Nichelle walked Akil out and when she closed the door she heard her cell ringing again. There was no doubt in her mind it was Renny. She leaned back against the door and put her head down. She hated that there was a big part of her that wanted to answer his call. That was the main reason she wanted to change her number. Nichelle knew in her heart that one day Renny would catch her at a vulnerable time and she wouldn't be able to resist. Even knowing he had a baby with Tierra couldn't completely shake the hold he had over Nichelle and it scared her.

"Supreme, I can't believe we're going to this event on Wednesday. You don't even like industry parties...never have," Precious commented as she changed the sheets on the bed.

"Well, it's not just any industry party. It's supposed to be an official affair. I am a businessman and it would be somewhat disrespectful not to show up. T-Roc supports a lot of my projects it would only be right I do the same."

"You not gonna get an argument out of me. I'm looking forward to putting on something fabulous and having a great time with my husband."

"You already know what you're wearing?"

"Not yet. I'm going to the city this weekend to find something fuckin' hot. You know the kind of outfit that's gonna make you wanna get me in the corner all night for a quickie," she laughed.

"Damn, I can't wait to see that outfit!"

"Speaking of outfits, I wish you could've seen Maya decked out in her prison gear. It was a far cry from the days when she raided my closet."

"I still can't believe you went to see her. Quentin must've given you some type of sob story to make that happen."

"It wasn't exactly a sob story. But I did want Quentin to know I was truly making an effort to have a relationship with him. He was so gung-ho about me seeing Maya and that's why I did it."

"Do you regret going?"

"No and yes. No, because I can now look Quentin straight in his face and tell him I did what he asked even though I can't stand that heffa. Yes, because it was a complete waste of my time. Maya, ain't remorseful about shit."

"Did you really think she would be?"

"Shit, the way Quentin was yapping, he almost had me convinced that she would be. Maya has really done a number on him. I don't understand how such an intelligent man can be taken in by that psycho. But then who am I to talk. I didn't realize Maya was the enemy until she was damn near about to put me under the grave."

"And don't forget how she played me. I have so much hatred towards Maya that I try to keep her and the entire situation that went down out of my mind. Because every time I think about it, I contemplate how I could have her killed and get away with it."

"Are you serious?"

"Damn straight."

"I never knew you felt that way. I mean I knew you were angry about what went down but you never told me you wanted her dead. I thought that was just me."

"Please. If Maya wasn't in jail she would be dead, I can promise you that."

"I know you feel that way but you really wouldn't have her killed."

"Yes I would! Why the hell not!"

"For one, as much as I detest her she is my sister."

"You're kidding right," Supreme chuckled. "Wait, you're not kidding. Are you really claiming that piranha as a relative?"

"Supreme, quit with the jokes. You know I'm not claiming Maya like that."

"That's what it sounded like to me."

"Listen, the fact is we are related and as much as I can't stand her, it would devastate Quentin if something happened to Maya. And I do care about him."

"That's noble of you, Precious. But I don't give a damn about how devastated Quentin would be if something happened to Maya. She kidnapped my daughter, she almost killed you and she manipulated me. Since Quentin loves his daughter so much, the best thing he can do for Maya is make sure she never sees the outside of that prison she's caged up in."

"Are you ready for the party?" T-Roc asked Genesis as he was going over some of the final details that the event planner sent over.

"Yeah, I'm ready for it to be over with so you can stop talking about it. You're fuckin' obsessed with this party."

"No I'm obsessed with perfection and I don't want any mishaps. After Wednesday everybody will know about my perfume and Nichelle."

"I can't believe I haven't met her yet. She's done two photo shoots and been in this office a few times but I always seem to miss her."

"Maybe if you weren't out on the streets playing Nino Brown and coming to work more often you would stop missing her."

"Funny but you have to admit I've been doing a lot better the past week."

"True, but how long is that going to last," T-Roc remarked sarcastically.

"Just like you run a multi-million dollar operation, so do I. I had to make sure some shit was in order before I focused a hundred percent on my business here. But we good now and I plan on devoting even more of my time to making sure shit is running smoothly over here. But I will tell you that from my observations I think you might be wrong about having a traitor on the inside."

"Really?"

"Yep, I think the problem is more so incompetence than betrayal. I noticed that some of the senior executives I've dealt with tend to let a lot of shit slip through the cracks because they're not being meticulous. They too busy taking bullshit lunches and being Hollywood that real shit ain't getting done."

"That's very interesting to hear," T-Roc said dropping the papers down on his desk that he was looking over and nodding his head.

"I'm telling you that's what's going down over here. See, my shit is handled in the streets and I don't have no choice but to check, double check and triple check my shit or else I can easily end up in jail, my paper fucked up or worse—dead. I don't have time to be Hollywood. I got the cops and these scheming ass street niggas to deal with. Your staff got these cushion ass jobs and they're more concerned about what they'll be charging next on the company credit card then closing the next big deal. You feel me?"

"Motherfuckin' right! But all that shit about to change. After I wrap this party up and it's the huge success I know it will be, I'm going in for the kill and cleaning house."

"That will serve you best."

"No doubt and of course I'ma need you to be here when I begin the process."

"I told you, I'm down for the cause. I have to make a quick trip to Memphis and I'm all yours."

"Memphis, what the fuck are you going there for and when? I know you not about to miss this party 'cause you gotta go to Memphis?"

"Hell no! I'm leaving Saturday night and I'm only staying for a couple days. I'll be back in time for the party on Wednesday."

"Cool. Go get all your shit worked out because when you get back I'ma need your full attention."

"And you will have it."

"So this is how it's gon' be for now on? No talking just dead silence between us," Tierra wanted to know as she stood in the kitchen, holding Elijah, warming up some baby formula for his afternoon feeding.

Renny continued reading his Bloomberg Business Week ignoring Tierra's question, which only made her try harder to get his attention.

"Here, feed the baby," she demanded, sitting down in what she knew Renny considered his private space. Tierra sat the baby bottle on top of some commerce magazines and newspapers that were piled up next to him. She continued to hold the baby since Renny hadn't looked up yet to acknowledge they were in his presence. It wasn't until Elijah started crying hysterically due to hunger that Renny finally spoke up.

"Aren't you gonna feed him?"

"No, you are."

"Tierra, I don't have time for your chicken-head games."

"Oh, so now I'm a chicken-head."

"No, you've always been a chicken-head."

"Well, this chicken-head is your baby mama so get over it."

"You're really trying my patience…now feed my son," he said handing the bottle to Tierra.

"You mean *our* son. I can't stop thinking about how Nichelle said you told her I was dead. Was that your intention, Renny, to kill me?" Tierra dangled her leg and fed Elijah, waiting to hear Renny's response.

"If I wanted you dead then you would be."

"Not necessarily because then who would feed your son," she mocked. "I'm thinking you were going to try and work shit out with Nichelle and then ease this baby situation on her once you had her wrapped around your finger again. Of course you would've never told her I was the mother and with me dead she would never find out. But me being the type of bitch I am, I fucked all that up for you."

"Tierra, since you have this all figured out, why are you running off at the mouth to me right now?"

"Because I ain't got nobody else to talk to and if I'ma be stuck in this crib wit' you, then the least you can do is keep me company."

"I'll be more than happy to take you back to my other place."

"I'm sure you would but Elijah wants to be around his dad and we get lonely being in that crib."

"I don't know what to tell you because I'm not your entertainment. I would prefer if you went back to the other place but if you're going to stay here, fine but don't bother me."

"I can't believe I let myself get in this fucked up situation. I always used to wonder what it would be like to have a baby by a rich nigga. I envisioned myself driving through my old hood, flossing in a fly ass whip, toting a fifteen-hundred dollar baby bag. I would be iced out and me and my kid would be dressed in nothing but top-notch designer shit. Instead, I'm sitting here in some boxer shorts, a dirty t-shirt, burping my son with a scarf tied around my head—this some straight bullshit!"

"When you made the decision to have the baby, I didn't promise you a damn thing. All I told you was that you and the baby would be taken care of. I'm doing my part. All that extra shit is some hoodrat street dreams that have nothing to do with me."

"I bet if Nichelle had your baby this would be a different conversation."

"Of course because the conversation wouldn't be with you. Nichelle is my girl, you're a very bad mistake. But Elijah is here now and I love him."

"Nichelle is not your girl, and now that she knows the truth she will never be your girl again. You need to get over that and focus on the family you have now, which is me and Elijah. I'm more your speed anyway. I'm a ride or die chick. You know that first hand since it was me you had doing a lot of your dirty work."

"Let me make this clear to you so you don't have any delusions about what this is. We share a child and once I get this Arnez situation resolved I will put you up comfortably and you can go on about your life which doesn't include me. I will see my son but I won't be seeing you. And in regards to Nichelle, you schemed behind my back to get her over here so she could find out about our little situation—mission accomplished. But I'll deal with Nichelle in my own way which I won't be discussing with you. Now you can excuse yourself because I want some alone time with my son."

Tierra handed Elijah over to Renny and left them alone. From a distance she watched their interaction and the reality of Renny only wanting a relationship with their son was clear. But it was a hard pill for Tierra to swallow. No, she wasn't in love with Renny, truth be told she didn't even like him but she was infatuated with the idea of having him as her man. He was fine as fuck, paper long, had street power and could lay it down in the bedroom although Tierra had only experienced that less than a hand full of times. Those were the sort of qualities that drew Tierra to Renny and made her fantasize about being his wifey or at least his glorified baby mama. Unfortunately for Tierra, Renny wasn't having any of it. But Tierra would not be deterred. She was determined to find a way to get in Renny's good graces and make him realize she was the sort of woman he needed on his team permanently.

Run This Town

Chapter 14

"Why are we going to Memphis again?" Genesis asked Nico as their Delta flight was about to take off.

"Yo, this like the third time you've asked me this same question."

"I keep forgetting what your answer was."

"That's what happens when you start getting up there in age."

"No, that's what happens when you work to fuckin' much. Between running shit on the streets and trying to maintain in the corporate world, that shit is exhausting on the brain."

"Ha, ha ha, that's funny."

"I'm glad you find it humorous, but seriously, why Memphis?"

"Like I told you before, Roscoe said that's where Delondo wants to meet. And since we need him for our Philly venture, we're taking our asses to Memphis."

"And who is Roscoe?"

"Damn, you ain't been listening to shit I've been saying. I'm surprised you showed up to this fuckin' flight."

"You picked me up, so I can't take credit for that."

"That's right. Roscoe is Delondo's right hand man. You know what you are to T-Roc."

"I told you about the jokes."

"The thing is I'm not joking. You know you gon' have to decide where your priorities are because you not gonna be able to juggle both the streets and working for T-Roc."

"I know. But it's like Jay-Z say, the game is a light bulb with eleventy-million volts and I'm just a moth, addicted to the floss. Eventually I'ma have to get out, no doubt about it."

"So you choosing the corporate world over the streets?"

"No, I'm choosing life over death or jail."

"Man, it don't have to be that way. We can do both. We gotta corporation ourselves. We keep running this shit like a machine ain't nobody gon' be able to fuck with us."

"I wanna believe you right. But this game cost me my best friend and my wife, so you gotta understand my apprehension. This gig with T-Roc will give me an opportunity to sleep a little better at night."

"Maybe, but will you be fulfilled? You ain't got to answer right now, just think about it. And even if you want to continue to do the T-Roc thing, CoCo can step up and take more responsibility. You know she'll be down for it."

"True, she's mos def a trooper."

"How's that working out anyway, you know mixing business with pleasure?"

"Much better than I thought it would. I'm actually considering getting serious with her."

"You mean, like making her yo' main girl?"

"Yep," Genesis said nodding his head. "Nobody can ever replace Talisa, but I think CoCo is the closest I'ma get."

"Damn, nigga, is you gon' wife her?" Nico sat up straight and leaned his head forward making sure he understood what Genesis was saying correctly.

"If I do decide we're going to be together I'ma do it right. I rather Amir see me married to a woman I'm living with then just shacking up. My son deserves to grow up and see that, you know like how it was supposed to be with me and his mother."

"Yeah, I feel you on that. Real talk, part of me be hoping Supreme will fuck up so bad that Precious leave his ass and we can get married and raise Aaliyah together as a family. That's fucked up right?"

"It's fucked up but I understand completely. You and Precious have a lot of history and out of that you all created a beautiful daughter. But she has a lot of history with Supreme too. You know you my man and I want you to be happy but it really does seem like the two of them are in love."

"I know, you're right. I have to accept that I'm her past and Supreme is her future."

When Genesis and Nico arrived downtown the first thing they did was check-in to their rooms at the Westin Hotel.

"Yo, what the fuck is going on down here," Nico wanted to know as the lobby was full of people.

"It looks like there's some sort of party going on. Why else would a bunch of black people be dressed up and circulating a hotel lobby on a Saturday night."

"Who knew Memphis had it poppin' like this. I see a couple of bad shorty's that I might need to keep me company while we're here."

"Nico, this is a business trip…remember."

"So I can't have no fun?"

"Fun, will come in the form of closing this deal with Delondo."

"True. I just wasn't expecting to come to Memphis and see it jumpin' like this. It messed up my train of thought for a moment. But I'm good because you're right, this is a business trip and business always comes first, speaking of which, this Roscoe calling me now."

"What's good man?"

"Everything, you and your partner here?"

"Yep, we're checking in our hotel now."

"Where you staying?"

"The Westin."

"A'ight. I'll be there within the hour to pick y'all up. I'll call you when I'm outside."

"Cool, we'll see you soon."

"Here, this yours," Genesis said, handing Nico his room key.

"Thanks, what you 'bout to get into?"

"Nothing, we 'bout to handle our business, wasn't that Roscoe on the phone?"

"Yeah, but he ain't gon' be here for about another hour. You wanna have a drink, maybe check out the party?"

"No, I'm going to my room and I advise you to do the same."

"Why you so uptight, relax."

"Fuck that. I gotta stay focused when I'm in Memphis. You know that nigga Antwon got popped here. CoCo and I had to do that little stint behind his bullshit."

"I didn't know the nigga got popped in Memphis."

"Yeah, fucking around with this connect at FedEx. You have no idea how much product go through these parts. It's right here in the middle of every fuckin' thing. I bet you that's why Delondo here, he 'bout to set up serious shop."

"Damn, and I always slept on Memphis. Shit they got hot bitches and you can make paper—this my type of town."

Precious was in the Gucci flagship boutique on 5th Avenue trying to find a showstopper for Wednesday's party when she noticed two women walking in her direction. At first, she didn't pay them any attention but as they got closer their faces looked mad familiar.

"Hey, Precious, I had no idea you were still in New York."

"Why would you. I mean it's not like we talk on a regular or at all for that matter." Normally CoCo would be ready to go in on a chick for being slick with the mouth like that, but she knew that was just Precious' style and not to take it personally.

"Good point, you remember Chantal," CoCo continued quickly moving on to the next topic.

"Vaguely."

"My daughter Justina has been begging to see Aaliyah again ever since her birthday party. We have to set up a play date for them."

"We don't live in New York. Our home is actually in LA."

"Oh, we have a mansion in Beverly Hills. So the kids can play together on the East or the West Coast."

"And who are you again?"

"Chantal, I'm T-Roc's wife." Chantal flashed her left hand showcasing the massive rock on her ring finger.

"How cute, I mean the ring that is. Not quite as big as mine, but still cute," Precious smiled, flashing her own, even more massive rock.

"Like I was saying, we really should set up a play date. Justina is so shy. She rarely ever likes anybody but she simply adores that Aaliyah and I like for my daughter to have what she wants."

Precious initially wanted to tell this life size Barbie doll with her blonde highlighted hair and perfectly applied makeup to get the fuck out her face but then she remembered the conversation she had with Supreme. He said he was a businessman and that T-Roc was somebody he fucked with. This was T-Roc's wife so she thought it was best to play the game.

"Let me get your number, I'm sure Aaliyah would love to play with Justina. It's like you said, our girls should have what they want." As Precious put Chantal's information in her phone she caught the frown on CoCo's face. Precious knew CoCo was probably surprised that she didn't give Chantal shade but it wasn't just about her anymore. She was a wife and mother and sometimes you had to make certain sacrifices for the sake of family, which included fucking with fake ass bitches.

"Wait until I tell Justina, she is going to be so thrilled."

"Are you ready to go, Chantal," CoCo asked ready to break the fuck out.

"Yes, see you at the party, Precious, and good luck finding something to wear because I simply couldn't find a thing to my liking," Chantal said before making her exit with CoCo.

Before Precious could start talking shit about Chantal in her head, she heard her cell ringing. "Hello."

"Hello, how are you?"

"I'm good, how are you?"

"Great, did I catch you at a bad time?"

"No, I was just trying to find something to wear for this party I'm going to."

"You talking about T-Roc's party?"

"Well damn, is everybody in the world going to this party?"

"Just about. From what I understand it's the hottest ticket going right now."

"Aren't you a little too old to be using words like hottest ticket going?"

"I'm your father not a dinosaur."

"So does that mean you'll be in attendance at this

soiree?"

"Unless something comes up, yes I will be there. So I hope you'll save me a dance."

"A dance with my father, I think that's an excellent possibility."

"Then I will definitely be showing up. That's actually one of the reasons I called you. I wanted to thank you for showing up and seeing Maya."

"I told you I would."

"You did, but I wasn't sure. I haven't had a chance to speak with you and see how it went."

"Quentin, I'm sure you've already spoken to Maya and she let you know exactly how it went."

"Yes, I have spoken to Maya but she didn't say much except how much she appreciated me getting you to come see her."

"That trick got so much game with her," Precious said, rolling her eyes as she browsed through the overpriced garments in the Gucci boutique.

"Given your comment, I'm assuming things didn't go that well."

"It went exactly how I knew it would. Maya is full of shit and is a manipulative monster—enough said."

Quentin let out a deep sigh, and for a slight second Precious felt somewhat guilty. "I hate you feel that way. I was hoping you and your sister could make peace."

"It's never going to happen."

"Maybe when she's released from jail and you all can sit down and talk you'll change your mind."

"Outta jail! What the hell are you talking 'bout? Maya

got a long bid on her hand."

"Not necessarily. I have the best lawyers in the country trying to get her verdict overturned."

"On what grounds?"

"Several and they believe it could happen, much sooner than I anticipated."

"Quentin, Maya deserves to be in jail! Why the fuck would you try and get her out," Precious screamed into the phone. Precious noticed several customers staring in her direction but she was too upset to care.

"People deserve second chances."

"Says who?"

"Nico. I mean that's what he gave you after you set him up to be behind bars for the rest of his life. And then you gave him a second chance after he shot you and left you for dead."

Precious tossed the clothes she was holding on the floor and stormed out the store. "What the fuck are you talking about? Why are you listening to the foolishness that is coming out of Maya's mouth?"

"Maya didn't tell me about what happened between you and Nico, he did."

"I don't give a fuck who told you. It doesn't change what Maya did to me and my family."

"I understand that but all I'm saying is that you shouldn't be so hard on your sister. People deserve another chance just like the one you were given."

"I let Maya keep her life. That's the best chance you can give anybody. If you want to have a relationship with Maya, that's your prerogative but trying to get her out of jail when she needs to do the time is another story. That is absolutely not cool with me."

"You've made your position clear but she's my daughter too."

"Then you need to decide which daughter you're backing in this situation."

"Are you asking me to make a choice between the two of you?"

"I'm telling you to make a choice because if you get Maya out of jail, we're done." Precious ended the call without so much as a goodbye.

"Nigel, do you have everything in place for Wednesday?" Arnez questioned as he stared out the window taking in his view of Manhattan.

"Yes, everything is covered."

"I don't want any fuckups."

"You won't have any. At this time next week, Genevieve will be in your custody."

"Indeed she will."

"Once you get her, are you going to continue your relationship with that Veronica woman?"

"You know, Nigel, I haven't decided yet. She's good in bed but a little too eager and dumb for my taste. But she could continue to be helpful so I might need to keep her around, if only temporarily."

"I feel you and you don't want her to get suspicious."

"That don't matter. Even if she did get suspicious, by that time it would be too late. I'll already have what

I want and her services will no longer be needed. But don't you worry about Veronica. Focus on making sure my plan is executed without a single flaw or you should worry about where you'll be this time next week."

When Roscoe took Genesis and Nico to a lounge on Beale Street to meet with Delondo they didn't know what to expect. It was a Saturday night, and the place was loud and crowded. Neither one understood why he chose this location for a business meeting since they wouldn't be able to hear shit anyway. Then Roscoe escorted them upstairs to what seemed to be some sort of secret room that the general public didn't know existed. When they entered there was a full shelf bar, a couple of waitresses and only a few plush couches for a select group of people to sit on. Since the hush-hush room was practically empty, they figured the man sitting on the corner couch had to be Delondo.

"Have a seat," Delondo said without looking up. Genesis and Nico looked at each other and then sat down. "Would y'all like something to drink?"

"No we're good." Genesis answered for both of them.

"Roscoe tells me y'all are looking to do some business," Delondo casually said still not looking at either of them.

"No offense but I don't do business with anybody who can't look me in my eyes when speaking to me. Nico you ready?" Genesis asked, standing up ready to go. Nico wasn't expecting for Genesis to go there but being a team player he stood up and followed his lead. Delondo then stood up too.

"No offense taken. I apologize, that was rude of me. I'm Delondo," he said extending his hand.

"I'm Genesis and this is Nico. And yes, we're trying to do business with you."

The three men sat down and Genesis got right to it. "We want a spot that you have in Philly. In exchange for clearing your men out and giving us no problems we can give you a rate on a product that nobody will be able to beat."

"I had Roscoe test out the product you gave him and I ain't gonna front, the customers went crazy."

"Our shit is the real deal. This would be a win-win situation for both of us."

"I agree. But I want to make sure that if I let you in you won't get greedy and try to take over all of Philly. I did some research on you, Genesis, and I know Philly was your main playing ground before you got caught up in some shit."

"You right it was and I know how profitable it is. But there's no need to be greedy. There's more than enough money to be made in Philly for all of us. I give you my word that I won't try to make any new moves on Philly territory without discussing it with you first. I don't want a war. I'm just trying to do profitable business."

"Good because you know how quick shit can get ugly in this business. The last street war I was in almost cost me my entire team. I don't want those types of problems again."

"I'm assuming you're speaking about your beef with Arnez."

"That's right," Delondo answered lifting up his head, "I guess you've done your research too."

"Arnez is on my enemy list too. But he's a hard cat to find."

"Maybe that's something else we can work on together."

"No doubt because I won't ever have any peace until I locate Arnez."

"Genesis, I see we have more in common than I thought."

"Me too. I think we will take you up on your drink offer after all," Genesis said eying Nico.

Spotlight
Chapter 15

When Nichelle hit the red carpet, the flashing lights almost blinded her. She had watched a scene like this play out on television but never did she imagine one day it would be her in this position.

"This way, Nichelle!"

"Over here, Nichelle!"

"Turn this way, Nichelle!" That's what she heard the photographers scream out over and over again. She watched Akil stand to the side, smiling as if he was so proud of her. Nichelle posed, taking each picture like a pro. But she was relieved when her publicist decided that she had taken enough pictures and swooped in to take her inside the party.

"You were great out there," Akil whispered in her ear.

"Wow, I can't get over how great it looks in here!" Nichelle commented, glancing around the venue that had a fantasy dreamland décor. The lavish space was turned into a cream labyrinth with an immaculate orchid display, black dance floor and black chandelier. There were flashing lightening strikes on the wall that went from a midnight thunderstorm theme into a beautiful sunset. "This place looks simply incredible," Nichelle kept saying over and over again.

"I told you T-Roc was going all out," Akil said, not at all surprised by how lavish the place was.

"Wait! Is that Sade up on stage singing?" Nichelle gushed. Akil simply nodded his head in acknowledgment. "There is no freakin' way Sade is performing at my party. This evening is already starting off beyond incredible, if only my mother was here to see how far her little girl has come." Nichelle felt tears swelling up in her eyes and swiftly shook them off. She wanted to enjoy her evening and not get burdened down with pain from her past.

"Nichelle, you look absolutely stunning tonight," T-Roc said when he seemed to appear out of nowhere.

"Thank you. I was told you specifically had this dress designed for me."

"I did and it fits you to perfection." T-Roc was accurate with his statement. The plunging v-neckline with side drape and dropped waist, hugged every curve on Nichelle's body. The beading and embroidery detail that cut diagonally across from front left chest to right hem gave the nude silk dress the illusion of contour lingerie.

"I'm glad you're pleased."

"Pleased is an understatement. I can't wait to show you off tonight. But I want to start by introducing you to my right hand man. I'm not sure he's arrived yet but he's been dying to meet you. Follow me." T-Roc grabbed Nichelle's hand and whisked her off into the awaiting crowd.

"Say what you want about T-Roc but that man sure knows how to throw a party," CoCo said to Genesis as they maneuvered through the crowd.

"This night was very important to him. It seems to be turning out better than even he imagined. I thought with that long ass line outside it would be dead in here but that's far from true. I believe everybody that received an invitation showed up and then some."

"You ain't lying." When Genesis and CoCo made it through the crowd they smacked right into Precious and Supreme who were holding hands like a young high school couple in love.

"Precious, it's good to see you and hello to you, Supreme," Genesis said politely.

"It's good to see you too. Hello, CoCo," Precious said dryly. CoCo gave her a half grin.

"Precious, excuse me for one second. I see somebody I need to speak to for a minute."

"Okay, I'll be right here." When Supreme wandered off, Precious turned her attention back to Genesis and CoCo. "So y'all having a good time?"

"We only got here a few minutes ago. It took forever to get in. The line outside is out of control. Luckily T-Roc had one of his assistants working the door and when she saw me standing in line she let us right in."

"Yeah, it was funny because I peeped some of those so called A-list celebrities giving us mad heated glares 'cause they didn't understand how we walked right in but yet they were still behind the velvet rope," CoCo chimed in.

"That makes it evident that it's not who you are but

who you know," Genesis said to both Precious and CoCo. Right then, Chantal came up and she began engaging in a conversation with CoCo. Of course she gave Precious a fake smile and wave while doing so. Precious didn't have time to think much of it because in came Nico and Quentin who made a beeline straight towards their growing circle.

"Man, I was wondering when you were going to get here," Genesis said to Nico when he walked up.

"Yo, it's bananas out there. Quentin suave ass is the one who got us in here so quick." After saying hi to both CoCo and Chantal, Nico made his way over to Precious. "You look absolutely beautiful tonight."

"Thank you. You look very handsome yourself, but then you always cleaned up nice."

"Don't nobody fill out a tailored suit quite like me," he boasted.

"Nobody but my husband," Precious smirked.

"Where is Supreme anyway? If you were my wife I would never leave you alone."

"But I'm not. Besides Supreme will be back any minute, he saw a business associate he needed to talk to."

"I don't mean to interrupt but Nico if you don't mind can I speak to my daughter for a moment."

"Quentin, we don't have anything to talk about unless you've decided to dead this get Maya out of jail movement."

"Damn! Who is that?" Nico's question caused Precious and Quentin to halt their conversation and look at what had put so much excitement in his voice.

"There you are," T-Roc beamed when he saw Genesis. "I've been looking everywhere for you. I wanted to introduce you to the star of this entire party."

"You must be Nichelle," Genesis said reaching out to shake her hand. "I've been looking forward to meeting you."

"Nichelle, this is Genesis, my right hand man that I've been bragging on."

The room seemed to stop for Nichelle. When her hand locked with Genesis she stared deeply into his eyes and wouldn't let go. "Did I hear T-Roc correctly, your name is Genesis?"

"Yes, you heard him right. I'm Genesis, Genesis Taylor."

Precious watched as CoCo seemed like she was ready to drag the young beauty across the dance floor. Although she wasn't a fan of CoCo's she couldn't blame her. She thought the chick in Genesis' face was a bad bitch. Precious knew that if a girl who looked and was built like that was holding onto the man's hand, that she wanted to make hers, she'd be heated too.

It seemed everybody was trying to be up in their conversation wanting to know what the two were talking about, especially CoCo. The longer Nichelle held onto Genesis' hand the more he began to be drawn into her. At first Nichelle's never ending grasp on his hand perplexed him but now he was feeling so much more, like some sort of connection but he didn't comprehend why.

"My name isn't Nichelle."

"Excuse me," he asked leaning forward to better hear what Nichelle said. With the crowd continuing to grow and the music getting louder it was hard for Genesis to understand what she was saying.

"My real name isn't Nichelle," she screamed out. "It's Gene…" but before Nichelle could get her name out the entire party erupted in chaos. The sound of bullet shots ripped through the air. As partygoers ducked, trying to hide, making sure they weren't an unfortunate casualty, the lights flickered and then the room went pitch black.

"Nichelle, where are you?" Genesis called out as he realized her hand was no longer interlocked with his.

"Everybody remain calm," T-Roc yelled to the crowd although he couldn't see shit. Paranoia ensued and you could hear glass breaking, tables being knocked over and screams of fear echoing through the room.

"Precious, are you okay," both Quentin and Nico yelled out in unison.

"Yeah, I'm fine. But what the fuck is going on and please let Supreme be okay," Precious huffed, hating feeling so helpless.

"I'm sure Supreme is fine. We all need to stay together until we figure out what's going on," Quentin said being the voice of reason.

"Nichelle," Genesis continued to call out. "Does anybody know where Nichelle is?" Then T-Roc called out to her but there wasn't any response. At this point both Chantal and CoCo were sick of their men being concerned about the next chick and not checking on them.

"I don't know where this Nichelle girl is, but your wife is fine, just in case you care."

"Chantal, of course I care. Are you okay?"

"I'll be much better when these lights come back on."

"I think we all will be."

"CoCo, is that you?"

"Yes, did you find your little friend yet?" Genesis ignored CoCo's question as he could hear the tartness in her voice and he wasn't in the mood. He felt compelled to make sure Nichelle was safe as if he was supposed to protect her.

It took another twenty minutes and then as if nothing had ever happened the lights suddenly came back on. The frightened crowd seemed reluctant to stand up as if they thought more bullets would start spraying the room.

"Precious, there you are…I was over there going crazy." Supreme was one of the first people bold enough to get up as he came running over to his wife. Once she saw her husband, Precious felt confident enough to get up too. She hugged Supreme relieved that neither one of them would need to go to the emergency room.

"Genesis, you locate Nichelle and I'ma find out what the fuck happened. Whoever is responsible for ruining this party, might as well consider themselves already dead." T-Roc stormed off like a man on a mission.

Nigel glanced to the backseat at a knocked out Nichelle. He smiled with pride at his accomplishment. His relishing was interrupted when he heard his cell ringing. "Hello," Nigel answered in an upbeat tone.

"All is well?"

"All is great!"

"That means things went smoothly."

"Yes. I should be at the location in less than an hour."

"Excellent. Make sure you take very good care of my guest. I want her in perfect condition before I kill her."

"Got you, boss."

Arnez hung up the phone and that feeling of content he had been yearning for had come at last. He obtained the coveted prize and he would use it to his full advantage. Arnez would use Nichelle to psychologically torture Genesis before killing her and sending her body parts to him piece by piece. He felt that was exactly what Genesis deserved. In his mind Genesis stole the only woman he ever loved in Talisa, then the baby she was carrying that he felt should've been his wasn't. Finally, he killed Chanel. The only woman that loved him for the disturbed monster he was. Arnez didn't have anybody and he wanted Genesis to feel as alone as him.

When Genesis and CoCo arrived back to their hotel room the mood was gloomy. Genesis seemed to get lost in his own world and wouldn't let CoCo in.

"Genesis, what is going on with you? You're acting panic stricken over a girl you met tonight for the very first time. You would think she was your long lost lover or something. But then again, she was probably still in pampers when you started gettin' your fuck on."

"CoCo, what the hell are you talking 'bout! Why does everything have to be about sex? It's not even like that. I'm not even attracted to her like that!"

"Yeah right! What, you think I somehow lost my

vision at the party. Every man in that spot with a working dick was attracted to that chick."

"Then I'm not every man because I have zero sexual attraction to Nichelle. But I am worried about her. She's vanished and something feels terribly wrong about that."

"Maybe she snuck out for a secret rendezvous. I'm sure she had more than enough willing takers."

"Jealously really doesn't look good on you."

"That's what happens...." Genesis put his finger up, cutting CoCo off when his phone began ringing.

"T-Roc, do have any news about Nichelle?"

"No. Nobody saw anything. Akil has been calling her but she's not answering her phone. We went by her apartment but she's not there. I think Nichelle might've been targeted."

"What! Why would you say that?"

"Because not only was nobody shot at the party, we did a thorough check of the room and the only bullets found were in the ceiling."

"So the bullets were fired up in the air?"

"Yes, I believe it was just a distraction to cause a big hoopla so whoever orchestrated this bullshit could use the opportunity to take Nichelle."

"But why and who?"

"Akil confided in me tonight that a couple of months ago somebody tried to kidnap Nichelle but he saved her before shit went sour. That's why he hired that bodyguard."

"You think that person is behind what went down tonight?"

"It's a serious possibility. Whoever it was they went

through a great deal of trouble to make sure this shit went out without a hitch. They were able to infiltrate security. This was too professionally executed to be some amateurs. That means the mastermind behind this got money and some clout."

"We need to find out everything we can about Nichelle and why somebody would want to kidnap her."

"I'm already on it."

"I do remember one thing."

"What's that?"

"She told me her real name wasn't Nichelle."

"Huh?"

"I know it sounds bizarre but the last thing I heard her say was that Nichelle wasn't her real name. Why she told me that, I don't have a clue. Before she could continue the chaos broke out."

"I'ma speak to Akil and see if he knows anything about that. I'll keep you posted."

"Do that." Genesis ended the call and sat down on the bed. "I knew something didn't feel right."

"What did T-Roc say?"

"He believes what happened tonight was some elaborate concoction to get at Nichelle."

"But she's just a model. Why would somebody go through all that trouble to get at her?"

"Apparently somebody thinks she's extremely valuable and I need to find out why."

Chapter 16

"Akil," I'm surprised to see you," Veronica said when she opened her apartment door.

"Sorry to pop up like this but we needed to see you. This is T-Roc and Genesis."

"Hello to both of you, please come in." The three men entered Veronica's apartment and she closed the door. "T-Roc, we've spoken a couple times on the phone during the contract negotiations for Nichelle. I hope everything is working out well with that. Nichelle invited me to the launch party but I wasn't feeling well and unable to make it. I'm sure it was a huge success."

"I suppose you haven't heard what happened?" T-Roc said to a baffled looking Veronica.

"No, this medicine my doctor gave me has had me out of it for the last couple of days. Why, what happened?"

"We believe Nichelle was kidnapped."

"What! When?"

"The night of the party. Shots were fired, the lights

went out and Nichelle hasn't been seen or heard from since."

"Oh my gosh, that's crazy," Veronica said putting her hand over her mouth in shock.

"We were hoping you might be able to help us," Genesis said, stepping forward.

"I'll do whatever I can but I don't know how I can help."

"You're her attorney, I'm sure you all have discussed many personal issues."

"Honestly, Nichelle was very private. I did feel like she was hiding some things but I could never get her to open up."

"Hiding things like what?"

"I don't know but there was definitely a wall up."

"Did she ever tell you what her real name was?"

"I assumed it was Nichelle, is that not the case?"

"We believe that's some sort of alias."

"This is getting stranger by the minute. Nichelle is such a sweet girl. I can't imagine anyone wanting to hurt her."

"We appreciate your time," Akil said, realizing Veronica had nothing to add that would be of any help.

"Of course. I wish I knew more. Please let me know if you find out anything."

"We will. Here," Genesis handed Veronica his business card. "Call me if you can think of anything. I don't care how simple it may seem."

"So what do you think?" T-Roc asked once the three of them was on the elevator.

"I think she was telling the truth."

"So do I," Akil added.

"But somebody has to know something but who."

"Genesis, I'm glad you're helping out so much with this but I have to admit I'm a little surprised you seem to be taking it so personally. I mean you hardly even know Nichelle."

"That's the thing, I feel like I do. In that brief encounter I had with her it's like I've known her forever. It's buggin' me out."

"Hey, man, I understand. She makes me feel the same way. Sometimes I have to remind myself that she's not my woman," Akil confessed.

"No! It's like I told CoCo, it's not that kind of feeling. Yes, there's no denying that Nichelle is a beautiful young lady but I'm not drawn to her out of lust. It's something much deeper than that."

"Like what? Now you got me curious," T-Roc admitted.

"I don't know but I believe once we find Nichelle it will all become clear."

For the last few days Nichelle had been going in and out of consciousness. Per Arnez's orders, Nigel kept her on a powerful sedative that had Nichelle in a deep sleep most of the time. During one of the times she came too she could hear what sounded like a heated argument between a woman and a man. She grabbed on tightly to the bed post trying to get her balance. She desperately wanted to get closer to the door so she could hear exactly what was being said. The sedatives being pumped in her system had Nichelle fucked up but her determination to find out what the hell was going on was stronger.

When she reached the door, of course it was locked. It didn't matter because she could hear what was being said as clearly as if she was standing in the room and part of the conversation. The words flying around had her astounded and petrified. It was worse than Nichelle could've imagined. When she heard the argument come to an end and the woman leave, Nichelle hurried back to the bed. She pretended to be asleep as she heard the doorknob turning.

"Nichelle, it's time to wake up. You need to eat," she heard a man say. He didn't sound like the same person that had been keeping her drugged and fed but clearly he knew her schedule, because like clockwork he visited her room each day at the same time. Nichelle could feel the man standing over her and breathing in her space so she acted as if she was beginning to wake up. When she opened her eyes to her horror it was Arnez breathing down on her. Her eyes widened in fear which brought a smile to Arnez's evil face.

"I knew it was you behind this."

"Of course you did."

"What are you gonna do to me?" Nichelle asked although she already knew his intentions. She heard Arnez plainly spell it out to the woman he was arguing with. But she still asked, there was no need in him knowing that.

"When the time is right, you'll know everything. For

now all I want you to do is rest. I'll bring your food in shortly and then give you your medication so you can go back to sleep."

"I'm not hungry."

"You've been behaving so well, don't get difficult," he said stroking Nichelle's hair. If you listened to the tone of Arnez's voice he appeared to be calm and sounded as if he cared about her well being which made him all the more sinister to Nichelle. "Now would you prefer water or juice with your meal?" All Nichelle could do was turn her head and cry, thinking about the plight her life had taken.

"Fuck!" Renny barked so loudly it woke the sleeping baby.

"What the hell is wrong with you? You woke up Elijah!"

"Arnez has Nichelle."

"Are you sure?" Tierra's voice filled with terror. Even though they were no longer close, Tierra still loved Nichelle like a sister and knowing Arnez had gotten his hands on her had her shook.

"Yes, the news is slowly leaking on the streets. The dude Arnez hired to do the shit is so fuckin' gitty he's running around bragging to motherfuckers."

"Has he told people where she's at?"

"No. But I got my people following him. If he don't lead them to Nichelle then I'll have them snatch his ass up and beat it out of him."

"Poor Nichelle, she must be so scared right now. There

has to be something more we can do, Renny."

"I'm working on it!"

"You should've moved on Arnez a long time ago. You know he's gonna kill her, right."

"Tierra, shut the fuck up! I don't need to hear this shit from you. I'm stressed as it is!"

"I didn't even know stress was in your vocabulary. You always acting like you got everything under control. Now Nichelle probably somewhere being tortured as we speak."

"If one strand of Nichelle's hair is out of place when I find her, Arnez won't know what the real definition of torture is until I'm done with him."

"Have you found anything new about Nichelle?" CoCo asked Genesis when they met up for a late lunch.

"No, and please don't pretend like you care."

"I deserve that. I'll admit, I let my insecurities get the best of me."

Genesis gazed up at CoCo, "Your insecurities. That's what has you trippin' over Nichelle?"

"Yes. Genesis, you know I'm in love with you but for whatever reason you don't want to make a commitment to me. When I see you fawning over a young beautiful girl like Nichelle it makes me feel like I'll never be the one."

"First of all, I wasn't fawning over Nichelle but I do care about what happens to her. And secondly, you are the one for me."

"Do you mean that?"

"Yes. I've felt that way for a long time now but with

so much going on it never seemed like the right time to tell you."

"Genesis, hearing you say that means everything to me."

"I should have told you sooner. I'm so used to thinking of you as my strong secure partner, that I forget you're also a sensitive woman. I apologize, you deserve more than that from me." Genesis reached over the table and took CoCo's hands, "You forgive me?"

"You don't even have to ask. And Genesis, I'll do whatever I can to help you find Nichelle. If she's that important to you then she's important to me too."

"You're incredible. Once I figure it all out then I'm going to focus on us. I was thinking maybe we could do the whole marriage thing, how does that sound to you?"

"Genesis, don't play with my emotions like that."

"I'm not. I want you to be my wife. The more crazy shit happens the more I want to get my priorities straight— which starts with family. I think that's why I'm so drawn to Nichelle because she reminds me…" Genesis stopped himself mid sentence and dropped CoCo's hands.

"Genesis, what is it?"

"She reminds me of the sister I never had, but she is my sister. That's what she was trying to tell me. She said her name isn't really Nichelle because it's actually Genevieve."

"You think Nichelle is your sister Genevieve? But why wouldn't she have told you that? You've been working with T-Roc for some time now."

"Because she didn't realize it until T-Roc introduced me. That's why she held my hand like that and asked me to repeat my name. She had been searching for me the same way I had been searching for her."

"Genesis, I'm not trying to rain on your parade but don't you think you might be reaching with this. That would be somewhat short of a miracle if it was true."

"It is true. I couldn't fully comprehend it until I started talking about family to you. That's why I felt this strong connection like I was supposed to protect her. She's my baby sister."

Chapter 17

"Arnez, it's so good to see you, and thanks for the beautiful flowers," Veronica said giving him a hug. "I've missed you."

"I missed you too."

"I'll be right back. I'm going to put these flowers in a vase and some water." As Arnez put his keys on the table next to the door he noticed a business card. When he picked it up he had to do a double take. "These are simply beautiful. They're going to look great on this table."

"Veronica, who is Genesis Taylor?"

"Excuse me?" she asked as she centered the flowers on the cocktail table in the living room.

"When I was putting down my keys I noticed this business card. Call me nosey but I wanted to see who it was that left their card with you. Do you have a new friend?"

"Oh, Arnez, no need to be jealous, he's a friend of my client Nichelle. It's horrible. She was kidnapped from that party I wanted you to attend with me. Such a young, sweet girl with her whole life ahead of her, I pray nothing bad has happened to her."

"So why did this Genesis guy come see you?"

"Like I said, he's a friend of hers and he also works with T-Roc. They've invested a lot of money in her I'm sure they want her back safely. It's a shame. I'm hoping that it isn't a kidnapping that maybe Nichelle just needed to get away."

"What do they think?"

"They're adamant it's foul play. That's why that Genesis man left his card. He said if I can think of anything to give him a call. But like I told him, Nichelle was guarded. I really don't know much about her. They did say that Nichelle may not even be her real name. It's all so bizarre."

"Have you been in touch with Genesis?"

"For what, I don't know anything although I wish I did. But if somebody did take that poor girl I hope they bury him under the jail cell. But enough with all these questions, you're beginning to sound more like a prosecutor than a boyfriend," Veronica laughed before giving Arnez a kiss.

"Boss, you're not going to believe who I just saw go into Veronica's building."

"Who?"

"Arnez."

"You think he was there seeing her?"

"I can't answer that but I think it's worth looking into."

"I agree. Find out what you can and keep me posted.

If Veronica is fucking around with Arnez that needs to be handled."

Delondo had decided to have Roscoe keep a watchful eye on Veronica after his last visit. Her behavior seemed more off than usual and she appeared to be acting strangely. After all the shit that went down with Denise he tried to be proactive when it came to seeing what his women friends were up to. He had way too much to lose and didn't want or need any surprises.

Delondo figured Veronica was seeing other men and he really didn't care since he wasn't checking for her to that degree. But never did he think she would be sleeping with his enemy. Then again, that's why he now always kept one eye open. He found out first hand through Denise how slick and sneaky women could actually be.

When Precious got out the shower she remembered she needed to call Supreme's parents and let them know she would be picking Aaliyah up in the morning. As she was about to dial their number, the loud screaming startled her to the point she almost dropped the phone. Recognizing the voice being that of her husband Supreme, Precious stopped being startled and was more interested in what and who had her husband so upset.

"I told you to only call me on this phone if it was a fuckin' emergency!"

"I've called you several times on your cell phone

and you haven't answered or returned my call. I had no choice."

"You always have a choice. What if my wife had answered?"

"Then I would've hung up. I'm not trying to cause any problems in your happy home, Supreme. But you've been impossible to get in touch with."

"I've been busy."

"I understand but I need to see you."

"Arnez, you have to wait. I got a lot of shit going on right now."

"Does that mean you don't need me to handle the Nico situation for you any longer?"

"What that means, is that I need you to get the fuck off my phone."

"Then meet me in an hour at our location in Jersey."

"Fine." When Precious heard Supreme slam the phone down she hung up on her end. Her mind was doing somersaults. *Could that be the same Arnez that Genesis has beef with. The one who had his best friend murdered and he believe his wife too. No, can't be. The same Arnez that Maya was running around with and who also killed Devon. But why would Supreme be associating with a killer and drug dealer like Arnez? Then what is this about handling the Nico situation? I have so many questions and no answers.*

"Precious, are you okay?"

"You scared me. I'm fine. But I do need to run out for a minute."

"At this time of night?"

"I'm having these crazy cravings. That time of the

month must be creeping up. I'ma stop at the grocery store, do you want me to bring you something back?"

"No, I'm good. I might be gone when you get back. I have to handle some business right quick."

"Okay, I'll see you when you get back home." Precious went in her closet and threw on some clothes with the quickness. She wanted to have ample time to get in her car and wait for Supreme to come out.

Precious pulled her car to the side of the road and within ten minutes Supreme was on his way out. She lingered briefly before following him to his destination. She tried to stay close enough so she wouldn't lose track of him but far enough away that he wouldn't realize she was tailing him. It wasn't an easy feat especially since she had no idea where he was going.

It took about thirty minutes but Supreme finally pulled up to a townhouse on a quiet street in Hackensack, NJ. Precious wrote down the address as she watched Supreme go to the door. From the angle she was looking it appeared a man opened the door and she assumed it was Arnez.

"I'm glad you were able to make it."

"Cut the bullshit, Arnez. With the stalking you were doing it was either I come to you or I would be taking the chance that you might show up at my front door next time. Then I would have to kill you. Now what do you want?"

"I have everything in place to move on the Nico situation."

"Then move. What the fuck are you telling me for?"

"I need some cash."

"What happened to the money I gave you a couple

weeks ago?"

"I had to use it for my other situation."

"Arnez, you're starting to become a burden to me and I don't like burdens."

"This is last time. Soon your problem will be resolved my problem will be resolved and we'll both be happy."

"I'll be in touch with you tomorrow. But, Arnez, this is it. If you don't get this Nico situation resolved once and for all you won't ever get another dime out of me."

When Precious saw Supreme exiting the townhouse she ducked all the way down. When he drove off, another man came out who looked to be black and Cuban. His face was somewhat familiar. "That has to be Arnez," Precious said out loud but wasn't certain. He got into a black SUV and Precious wrote down the license plate number before he drove off.

When Genesis woke up in the morning the first thing he did was call T Roc. "What time are you going to get to the office?"

"I'm on my way now."

"Good, then I'll see you shortly." Genesis wanted to share what was running through his mind with T-Roc because he was a thinker like him and could maybe give some informative insight. When Genesis was about to get in the shower he heard his cell ringing and was surprised at the number that came up. "Precious, how are you?"

"Good, how 'bout you?"

"I've been better but I'm sure we all have. But I'm sure

you didn't call just to see how I was doing."

"Actually, I was. I know you were pretty upset when you left the party last week. Did you ever find your friend?"

"As a matter of fact I haven't."

"Well I'm sure she'll show up."

"Yeah, I'm hoping so. Is that all you wanted?"

"I did have one other question for you."

"Ask it?"

"You recall when I was on that mission to find Devon because I wanted to locate Maya."

"Of course."

"I never got to speak with Devon because a man by the name of Arnez got to him first."

"Yes."

"I was talking to Quentin trying to tie up some loose ends with everything that happened during that period of time. We got in this little debate because I swear the Arnez that killed Devon is the same one Maya was running around with. I've never seen him but isn't Arnez black and Cuban?"

"Yes he is. But why are you really asking me about, Precious?"

"I just told you."

"Precious, you're a grown woman and I can't tell you what to do but I'm warning you. Don't cross paths with Arnez. He is a cold blooded killer."

"That's exactly what I was trying to explain to Quentin. Maya was running around with a notorious killer. Thanks for clarifying that for me." Precious ended her call with Genesis completely confused. In her heart she knew whatever involvement Supreme had with Arnez equaled no good. But if she warned Nico then she would be betraying her husband. If she didn't warn Nico she knew more than likely he would end up dead. When she saw Supreme coming down the stairs she felt her only option was to confront her husband.

"Good morning, baby. What time are you going to get Aaliyah?"

"I was hoping you could go get her. I have some errands I need to run."

"Wish I could but I'm swamped today."

"What do you have to do?"

"Bullshit work stuff."

"Does any of that bullshit have to do with Arnez Douglass?"

"Who?" Supreme didn't break a sweat when he acted as if he wasn't familiar with the name.

"Arnez, the man that called our house last night."

"Oh, him. He's going to do some minor contractual work for me."

"Stop with the bullshit, Supreme! Arnez is a killer and a drug dealer why are you fuckin' with him? Answer me, Supreme!"

"It's nothing. You always have to keep a couple of criminals on your payroll, nothing to concern yourself about."

"Don't patronize me. I know you've hired him to kill Nico." Supreme stopped what he was doing and glared at his wife.

"Who else have you told that to?"

"Nobody…yet."

"And you're not going to."

"Supreme, I will not let you kill Nico."

"Why do you fuckin' care! I'm your husband, me!" Supreme barked as he pointed his finger at his chest. "Fuck Nico Carter! He doesn't deserve to live!"

"That's not your decision to make. He has every right to live just like you and me. Who gave you the right to play God with his life?"

"He did, the day he shot you and killed my baby. Then I take his child from him so we can call it even, then what does he do. He finds out Aaliyah is really his daughter and comes to claim what should be mine and he doesn't even deserve."

"You always knew Aaliyah was his daughter, didn't you?"

"Of course. When I found out you slept with him when you thought I was dead I knew there was a significant chance so I had the blood test done. But even after finding out, I loved Aaliyah like she was my very own flesh and blood. But then that accident happened and you know the rest."

"If Aaliyah hadn't needed that blood transfusion you would've carried her true paternity to your grave?"

"What don't you understand? Nico took my child from me it was only right that I took his."

"I don't even know who you are."

"Yes you do. I'm Xavier Mills and you're my wife."

"If you have Nico killed that will change. I will not be married to a man that would kill Aaliyah's father. She loves him."

"I'm her father!" Supreme yelled out.

"Yes you are but so is Nico. You have to accept that just like he has to accept that you're her father too. Don't do this, Supreme. I can forgive you for just about anything but not that. I can't knowingly allow you to break our daughter's heart."

"I love waking up to you," Veronica whispered in Arnez's ear.

"And I love waking up inside of you."

"Isn't this cozy. My worst enemy dicking down my," Delondo paused for a few seconds. "I don't know what to call you, my ho?"

"Fuck you, Delondo! I knew I should've gotten my key back from you last time."

With swiftness Arnez slid out of Veronica and pressed his back against the headboard. "Delondo, this doesn't need to get ugly," Arnez said with cool, unshaken calmness.

"You all know each other?"

"No doubt. You thought he was just fuckin' you on a regular just because. There is always an ulterior motive when let's just say, Arnez has his dick in something. Tell her Arnez."

"Is what Delondo saying true?" she asked Arnez who wasn't saying anything. "But what would he want from me?" Veronica then directed her question to Delondo who seemed more than happy to answer.

"Information about me."

"Don't flatter yourself. I had put you on the backburner. I had more pressing issues to deal with."

"So what Delondo is saying is true, you were using me but for what?"

"Let me guess…Genesis."

"Genesis," Veronica echoed in bewilderment. "I don't know a…" Veronica caught herself and recalled the interrogation Arnez gave her when he spotted the business card that had Genesis' name on it. "You did ask me a bunch of questions about him. But he only came to talk to me because of my client Nichelle. I have no ties to Genesis."

"How can a woman be so brilliant in the boardroom but a complete dummy when it comes to using common sense," Arnez commented as he stared at Veronica.

"Don't be cruel, Arnez. You don't have to show out because Delondo is here. I know what we share is real."

"Veronica, I sought you out because I knew you were Nichelle's attorney. But being easy on the eyes and good in bed made it less of a hassle."

"You used me to get to Nichelle?"

"Ding…ding…ding. You're finally gettin' it."

"Was it you that had her kidnapped at the party?"

"Jackpot! That legal mind of yours is finally kicking in."

"And I'm the one who gave you all the information when we were at dinner that night. You bastard!! You used me to hurt that poor girl! I hate you!" Veronica began lashing out on Arnez with her fist.

"Veronica, calm down," Delondo said grabbing her arms. Now that he knew she hadn't sold him out, he felt kinda bad for her. She had caught real feelings for Arnez and he had simply played her out.

"You'll pay for this, Arnez! I promise you, you'll pay for this!" Veronica continued to scream."

"Maybe I will but it won't be by you." With all the commotion Veronica was causing, it was nothing for Arnez to retrieve the gun he kept under the pillow. Most women didn't know it but Arnez always kept heat in the bed. That was the only way he was able to sleep at night. By the time Veronica realized what was happening the rounds were already fired and a bullet was making its way through her temple.

Delondo acted with rapid speed and reached for his gat but he wasn't fast enough. The first bullet grazed his shoulder then next landed in his chest. He fell to the floor and Arnez watched as the blood gushed from both his victims. Knowing he didn't have time to waste, Arnez quickly dressed, grabbed what few belongings he had over and left. In his rush to exit, Arnez didn't realize he hadn't finished the job.

"T-Roc, excuse me for a minute. I need to take this call." Genesis left out of T-Roc's office before answering. "What's up, Delondo...hello...Delondo." Genesis pulled the phone away from his ear and looked at it to make sure there was a call.

"Genesis, can you hear me?"

"Barely, what's going on are you a'ight?"

"No, Arnez just shot me."

"What! Where are you?"

"Veronica's apartment. Listen, Arnez has Nichelle. I don't know who she is to you, but that's who has her... Arnez." Then there was silence.

"Delondo, are you there...Delondo!" Genesis rushed back in T-Roc's office. "Come on we have to get to Veronica's apartment."

"What happened?"

"I'll tell you on the way...let's go!"

Girl I Got You
Chapter 18

All morning Renny had been back and forth on the phone. Tierra knew it was about Nichelle but Renny was keeping tight-lipped. He wouldn't share shit with her and it was driving Tierra crazy. So when she caught the tail end of a conversation that Renny was having with whom she assumed was one of his workers she decided to act fast.

Tierra saw Renny jot something down on a notepad before going upstairs to take a shower. If what she heard Renny say was correct what he wrote down was the address where Nichelle was being held captive. In her attempt to be the savior and gain brownie points with Renny, Tierra decided she would be the person to rescue Nichelle. She copied the address down and then left Renny a note letting him know she stepped out, which technically she wasn't allowed to do. But the baby was sleeping, Renny was in the shower and if she was going to make a move it was now or never. She grabbed the keys to one of Renny's cars and off

Tierra went to play hero.

When Tierra pulled up to the townhouse she parked the car across the street and observed for a few minutes. There seemed to be no activity going on and she wondered if she was at the right place. Her gut told her she was and that is what Tierra decided to follow. When she got to the front door she tried to peep inside a slight opening in one of the windows. But again, there seemed to be no activity. She glanced around the quiet street again before picking up a huge rock that was nestled in some bushes. Tierra played with the doorknob one good time, knowing it wouldn't be unlocked. She then used her rock to bust open the glass and reach inside to unlatch the lock.

Tierra's heart was pumping as she walked around the sparsely furnished crib. She immediately started opening doors trying to see if Nichelle was being stashed in any of the rooms. When she came to a closed door at the end of the hall, she opened it up to see Nichelle's arms and legs tied up to the bed posts. Nichelle's body was so still that at first Tierra thought she was dead. But as she got closer she saw slight movement.

"Nichelle, wake up. It's me Tierra." Nichelle appeared to be so weak that it was evident to Tierra that they had her on some type of drug. She immediately began untying the ropes to free Nichelle from the bondage.

"Tierra, is that you," Nichelle mumbled, coming out of her daze.

"Yes, it's me, Tierra. Girl, don't you worry. I'ma get

you out of this dungeon and take you home."

"Where's Genesis?" Nichelle's voice was barely audible.

"Who! Genesis? Oh, your brother, that's right his name is Genesis. Baby girl, I don't know where your brother is but we can figure that out after I get you outta here. Now I'ma need you to work with me," Tierra said, trying to get Nichelle to stand up.

Tierra was tempted to look in the closet or the drawers to see if there were any clothes to put Nichelle in put she was feeling like she didn't have time for all that. Tierra decided the long nightgown Nichelle had on would just have to do.

"My legs are so weak."

"I know sweetie, but you have to be strong. We're almost in the clear." Nichelle was halfway walking and halfway being held up by Tierra. Tierra wanted to lift her up but she wasn't strong enough and she couldn't rush Nichelle because her legs kept buckling up. When they finally reached the passenger side of the car, Tierra was ecstatic. She had put in some work and was tired as a motherfucker.

"Tierra, thank you for saving me. You know I never stopped loving you," Nichelle said as she slumped over in the front seat.

"I know and I never stopped loving you either. We family, that'll never change," Tierra said, making sure Nichelle's seat belt was securely fastened.

When Tierra was ready to breathe a sigh of relief her eyes locked with Arnez as he was pulling up to the townhouse. At first he stared at her like he was seeing a ghost and then he jumped out his SUV, charging at her like a mad man. Tierra sprinted to the driver's side, struggling to put the key in the ignition. She knew Arnez was about to be up on her. When Tierra heard that engine start up, she put the car in drive, pressed down on the gas and hauled ass. From her rearview mirror she could see Arnez getting back in his SUV ready to come after them. Tierra was so caught up in watching what moves Arnez was making that by the time she realized her own moves were in jeopardy it was too late.

"Tierra, watch out," Nichelle screamed before Tierra slammed in the back of a garbage truck. The impact was so powerful the front passenger airbags deployed instantly. Nichelle might've been out of it before but that crash woke her the fuck up.

"Nichelle, are you okay?" Nichelle looked at Tierra and nodded her head.

"What about you, are you okay?"

"I'm okay," Tierra answered but something seemed off to Nichelle.

"Where's your cell phone? I'ma call for help."

"Do that, but, Nichelle."

"Yes, what is it?"

"Please take care of Elijah for me." And just like that, Tierra was dead.

"Tierra...Tierra, wake up. Tierra, this isn't funny, I need you to wake up." Nichelle reached her arm over and began shaking her friend but she wouldn't move. "Tierra, I don't want you to die," Nichelle cried out. "I'm so sorry for all the mean things I said to you. Please don't die, Tierra, please don't die."

"Save the pity party, you're coming with me," Arnez roared, yanking Nichelle out the passenger seat.

"Miss, are you and your friend okay," the driver of the garbage truck asked.

"Get back in your truck before it's you laid out dead," Arnez threatened waving his gun around. The driver backed up towards his truck not ready to die for being a concerned citizen.

"We need to get some help for Tierra," Nichelle pleaded.

"Tierra is dead! You need to be worried about yourself. Now get in the truck!" Arnez shoved Nichelle in the passenger side, slamming the door.

Reality kicked in for Nichelle. She was burnt out from all the sedatives in her system, the car accident, not eating properly and just being fucked up in the game. She was barefoot and draped in a nightgown. Her body was begging to go back to sleep but she knew this was it. Did she allow herself to simply die at the hands of Arnez or did she fight to live. With Nichelle looking unbelievably pitiful, Arnez had disregarded taking any precautions to make sure she didn't try and get away, which gave her a slight upper hand.

"I can do this," Nichelle mouthed under her breath before conjuring up enough strength to bounce. She waited for Arnez to get inside the driver's side and close the door. Then she quickly unlocked her door and dashed across the street.

"Get the fuck back here," Arnez growled, pounding his gun on the steering wheel.

The blazing hot cement ground had Nichelle squirming as she tried to make her getaway. She didn't know where she was running to but feeling grass under her feet would be a welcomed reprieve. When Nichelle came to a row of townhomes she started randomly ringing doorbells and banging on doors, but either nobody was at home or they didn't give a fuck to see what she wanted. As Nichelle dragged herself to the next property she noticed Arnez slowly cruising down the street. It was reminiscent of Arnold Schwarzenegger in Terminator when he was on the prowl ready to murk Sarah Connor.

Nichelle knew when Arnez spotted her because he started speeding up the street. She tried to limp away but it wasn't looking good for Nichelle—shit was critical.

"Unless you wanna die right here on this sidewalk, get back in this fuckin' truck." Arnez raised his gun out the window letting Nichelle know he was serious. Part of her would rather die in the hot ass sun on the sidewalk then willingly get in a truck with a man that was going to kill her no matter what. Right when Nichelle resigned herself to accept her demise, optimism showed its face in the form of Renny O'Neal.

Renny pulled his own truck right next to Arnez and got out. "Arnez, that's enough," he said shutting the door.

"If it isn't my favorite cousin. What are you doing here, Renny?"

"Putting an end to this bullshit. You've taken things way too far. It's time to let it go."

"I appreciate your concern, but this has nothing to do with you. You don't even fuck with that chick anymore. So

I suggest you get back in your truck and let me handle this."

"Nichelle is off limits to you. So I'ma make that same suggestion to you—back your truck up and get the fuck out of here…cousin." Renny walked over to Nichelle who was now lying on the ground hardly able to keep her eyes open. He knelt down and cradled her wilted body in his arms. Nichelle was so frail that it broke Renny's heart. He felt responsible for her predicament and promised himself he would make it right.

"I'ma need you to hand her over."

Renny looked up at Arnez who was now standing a few feet away with his gun pointed at him. "Arnez, what the fuck are you doing?"

"All I want you to do is hand Nichelle over and then you can go about your business."

"She is my business."

"Not anymore. This is bigger than some ex-boyfriend/girlfriend shit y'all have going on. This is business, Renny. You understand that."

"Yo, this fuckin' obsession you have with her brother has destroyed you. Let the shit go!"

"I can't do that. Genesis will be dealt with so I need you to hand me over his sister," Arnez continued not letting up on the solid grip he had on his gun. "You my favorite cousin…I love you, man, but I need you to get out the way so I can handle my business."

"You would kill your own blood for that bullshit you got going on wit' that nigga!"

"It's not personal," Arnez smiled and shrugged his shoulders as if to lighten the mood.

"Fuck you then." Without warning, Renny reached in the back of his pants for his gat and lit Arnez's ass up. Without giving it a second thought, he lifted Nichelle off the ground and laid her down gently in the back seat. Renny drove off leaving his cousin for dead like he was a piece of disposable trash.

Still Standing
Chapter 19

Nichelle woke up and the first person she laid eyes on was Renny. He was at Nichelle's bedside holding her hand. "Where am I?"

"At my place. How are you feeling?"

"I'm okay but my head hurts."

"Yeah, you have a little bump. The doctor said you have a minor concussion and would be in some pain."

"I saw a doctor, did I go to the hospital?"

"No, I had the doctor come see you here. He gave you a full check-up and left you some medication. You're gonna be fine."

"Thank you for taking care of me."

"You don't have to thank me. If anything I should be asking for your forgiveness."

"I do forgive you. You know what happened to Tierra don't you?"

"Yes," Renny answered somberly.

"I hope before she died she knew that I forgave her

too."

"Tierra knew how much you loved her."

"Before she died she asked me to take care of Elijah for her."

"How do you feel about that?"

"The question is how would you feel? He is your son."

"Nichelle, you've been through so much and a great deal of that is my fault. I don't want you to do anything you're not comfortable with."

"Elijah deserves to have a mother that loves him. Besides Tierra, I don't think another woman could love him as much as I would."

"You're amazing. I know I don't deserve to have you in my life but I can't let you go—I won't."

"You don't have to. If it wasn't for you Arnez would've taken me and I'd be dead. Whatever happened in the past, that's where it's gonna stay. But I do need you to do something for me."

"Tell me. Whatever it is, I'll make it happen."

"Get in touch with my brother."

"Nichelle, I wasn't lying when I told you I didn't know where Genesis was."

"I found him. I know exactly where he is. Call this number, he'll get you in contact with my brother."

"T-Roc, I don't know how much more of this I can take. We keep hitting one dead end after another. Veronica is dead, so even if she knew something she can't tell us. Delondo is going to pull through but I doubt he knows where Arnez has Nichelle. This shit is driving me crazy!"

"I know but times like this, it's important to remain calm."

"Do you think Nichelle is still alive?"

"Honestly, I hope so but when you're dealing with a deranged individual like Arnez it can go either way."

"You right and that's what's eating me up inside. If I lose another person at the hands of Arnez, I don't know what will become of me."

"Don't talk like that," T-Roc said putting his hand on Genesis' shoulder. "We'll get through this." Both men looked up when they heard a huffing Akil scurrying through the door.

"Man, you a'ight." Genesis was used to seeing Akil polished and unruffled. The haggard vibe he was giving off had him concerned.

"I just a received a call. Nichelle's been found."

"Is she alive?" Genesis stood up and swallowed hard. He was scared at what the answer might be.

"Yes, she is," Akil beamed, "and, Genesis, she's asked to see you."

When Genesis, T-Roc and Akil drove up the townhouse on the water front property there was an unspoken allegiance between the men. They had all shared in the search for Nichelle and now they celebrated in her survival.

"Are you going to knock on the door or what," T-Roc said playfully, sensing Genesis' nervousness. But he didn't have to because the door opened.

"I saw y'all pull up. Come on in, I'm Renny."

"I'm Genesis. This is T-Roc and Akil, who you spoke with on the phone. Thank you for calling."

"Don't thank me. Nichelle was adamant that I got in contact with you. All she's been saying is that she wants to see her brother."

The biggest smile crossed Genesis' face and it spread like it was contagious because the other men couldn't help but smile too.

"She's upstairs, the second bedroom on the left." Genesis followed Renny's directions and when he got to the bedroom he paused for a second before going in.

Nichelle scooted her still aching body up straight in the bed when she saw Genesis standing in the doorway. A smile and tears hit her face at the same time. "My brother, I've finally found my brother."

"Oh, Genevieve," Genesis sighed. I didn't know if I would ever see you again. Is it okay that I call you Genevieve?"

"You can call me whatever you like as long as you put sister somewhere in there."

"How are you, did Arnez hurt you? I put it on everything that he will pay for what he did to you."

"I'm fine and calm down. You don't have to worry. Arnez will never hurt anybody again."

"Why, what happened?"

"He's dead."

"Are you sure?"

"Yes."

"How did he die?"

"You promise you won't say anything?"

"Of course. One thing you don't ever have to worry about, what's between us and what we share will always remain between us."

"Renny saved my life and in the process he killed his cousin."

"Renny and Arnez are cousins?"

"Yes."

"Renny must love you a lot to kill his cousin for you. That should've been me saving your life."

"You have. When I lost our mother…"

"Our mother is dead?" Genesis asked cutting Nichelle off.

"Yes. Arnez was responsible for that too. Right before she died is when she told me about you."

"What? So all these years you never knew you had a brother?"

"No. When I was little our mother accidentally killed the man I thought was my father. We had to leave North Carolina so she wouldn't go to jail. We changed our names and got new identities. We cut off everybody from our past. But before she died, she wanted me to know about you and find you. She said you would protect me."

"This is all so much. But it makes sense and explains why I could never locate you all."

"But with everything that was going on with me I never gave up hope that I would find you. Then that night at the party when you told me your name was Genesis Taylor. I knew God answered prayers."

"I felt this connection to you and I couldn't figure out

why and then it hit me. Once it did, there was nothing that could shake me believing you were my sister. We have so much time to make up for. I want you to move in with me."

"Genesis, stop it," Nichelle laughed.

"I'm serious. I want to spend every day and night with you. Getting to know you, your favorite food, movie, music...everything."

"You're so sweet. You're going to be like the best brother ever."

"Nichelle, don't cry."

"I'm trying not to," she sniffled. "But I've lost so much but finding you makes up for all of it." Genesis reached over and held his sister so tightly. He loved her. He didn't know it was possible to love someone so much that he barely even knew.

Black Rose

Chapter 20

"So I'm finally going to meet your sister. I can't wait!" CoCo said as she set the table for dinner.

"Yep! I think y'all are going to get along great. She's wonderful," Genesis gushed. "I mean when you look at her she appears to be so delicate but inside of her she's a fighter, she's strong. She reminds me of Talisa that way. There was an awkward silence and then Genesis realized what he said. "That might've been a little insensitive of me, I apologize."

"Don't. There is nothing wrong with you comparing your sister to Talisa. I know how special Talisa was to you and you don't have to apologize for that."

"How am I so lucky to be surrounded by such amazing women," he said giving CoCo a long seductive kiss that instantly got her panties wet.

"I think you need to back up. Your sister will be here any minute and you don't want to start something you can't finish."

"True. But it's on tonight."

"I'm counting on it."

"Tomorrow I'm taking Nichelle with me to pick up Amir from Talisa's parents house. Do you want to ride with us?"

"What? You never let me go over there with you!"

"We're engaged now. I think it's time for them to be introduced to the woman who will be my wife and a mother to their grandson."

"Call me that again?"

"Call you what?"

"Wife. I like the way that sounds. I'll be Mrs. Genesis Taylor."

"Yes you will be. And being able to have my sister there is the best wedding gift ever. These last few weeks I've spent with her have been some of the happiest of my life. She's going to be a great Auntie to Amir.

Knock…knock…knock

"That must be Nichelle now," Genesis said going to the door.

"Hi," Nichelle smiled giving her brother a hug.

"Hey, I thought Renny was coming with you."

"Some business came up at the last minute. But if he doesn't finish up too late he'll stop by when he's done."

"That's okay. That means I don't have to share the two most important women in my life tonight."

"So CoCo's here? I can't wait to meet her."

"Yeah, she's finishing up the table now." Nichelle followed Genesis to the dining room. "There's my beautiful fiancé."

"Hi, CoCo. It's such a pleasure to meet you. Genesis has said nothing but wonderful things about you."

"Well, he hasn't stopped raving about you. You've made such a huge impact on his life."

"He's done the same for me too."

"Nichelle, can I get you something to drink?" CoCo offered.

"I can get it myself but thank you. I apologize for starring at you but you seem so familiar to me."

"Really, maybe it's from that night at the party."

"No, I don't remember seeing you there."

"I bet you met her twin sister Chanel before."

"Yes, I did meet Chanel with Renny at Arnez's crib and that night they shot Tierra. That's your sister."

"My sister is now deceased but I apologize for everything she did to you and your friend."

"Let's not talk about them. Tonight is about us and having a good time," Genesis said in effort to kill any negative vibes.

"You're right big brother. I'ma go in the kitchen and get something to drink. Can I bring y'all back anything?"

"No, we're good," CoCo said, pulling Genesis close to her. "Take your time. While you're in the kitchen, I'm going to try and get my fiancé to nail down a wedding date."

"You do that," Nichelle laughed, entering the kitchen. She opened the refrigerator and pulled out a bottle of Sparkling Cider. She listened as CoCo and Genesis went back and forth discussing their wedding plans. From the time she got a glass out the cabinet to then pouring the cider everything changed and would never be the same again.

"Nichelle, I told CoCo that you would be the perfect bridesmaid in our wedding. What do you think about that?" he asked when she came out the kitchen.

"It was you, CoCo." Genesis and CoCo looked at each other in confusion then back at Nichelle.

"It was me, what?"

"It was you that I heard arguing with Arnez when he had me captive in that townhouse."

"You're mistaken, Nichelle. I haven't seen Arnez since my sister died."

"When I saw you and I said you seemed familiar, it wasn't because of the way you looked. It was your voice. I'll never forget your voice and what you said! When I went in that kitchen and I couldn't see your face but just listened it all came back to me."

"Nichelle, calm down. I know that ordeal with Arnez was brutal for you but CoCo wasn't there it was somebody else."

"No, Genesis. It was CoCo. She was working with Arnez. They were arguing because she knew he was responsible for kidnapping me. They had a deal but he reneged." Genesis turned towards CoCo trying to get a read on the situation.

"Genesis, your sister was clearly traumatized by what Arnez did to her. You know how much I hate Arnez. I would never work with him."

"You're a liar! You said that you gave him all the information he needed to have Talisa killed. Then you said that Genesis killed your sister and if you could get over losing her then he would get over the death of a sister he doesn't even know. Your only beef with Arnez was that you wanted to make sure he didn't kill Genesis because you had earned the right to have him all to yourself. Isn't that how you put it?"

"Your sister is trippin'…this is crazy!"

"No, you're crazy!" Nichelle screamed, pointing her finger at CoCo. "Arnez said he planned to cut my body parts up and send them to Genesis. He said he wanted to torture him mentally but wouldn't kill him. You agreed! You went so far as to say that with first losing his wife and then losing his sister, Genesis would be so traumatized he would be totally dependent on you for emotional support."

"Genesis, if this is true why is she just now telling you?"

"The way they kept me drugged up and then the car accident, I had a minor concussion, so some of my memories were suppressed. But the doctor told me with time more and more things would slowly start coming back to me. And when I heard you in here with Genesis the dreadfulness I felt when you were talking to Arnez that day hit me all over again."

"CoCo, why? Why would do this?" Genesis voice seemed numb.

"Genesis, you believe her?"

"Why would Nichelle make it up and how does she know all of this if it didn't go down exactly the way she said?"

"It's no secret what happened to Talisa."

"True, but I never told her I killed Chanel. That was

between me and you."

Dismay crept over CoCo's face. She was busted. "Genesis, I was the only woman that was right for you but you could never see that until after Talisa died."

"You took away my wife. My son will never know his mother because you thought you were the only woman who was right for me. I don't know what to say to you."

"I do! If you and Arnez had your way, I would be dead. And my brother would've ended up being married to a piece of shit like you. You're sick!"

"Nichelle, I want you to go home. I'll call you later."

"I'm not leaving. I'm staying here with you."

Genesis slightly pulled Nichelle to the corner and spoke in a low tone. "I want you to go home. I'll handle things here with CoCo."

"Genesis, I don't want to leave you. Whatever you're going to do with CoCo, you can do it in front of me."

"You're my sister and I have to protect you. Certain things I don't want you to see."

"I think it's too late," Nichelle said shifting her eyes away from Genesis. Genesis turned to see what Nichelle was alluding to and saw CoCo holding her purse in one hand and her gun in another.

"Genesis, you know I never move without my Bitch. I hate it has to come to this but when you asked your sister to leave I knew what was up."

"I had no intentions of harming you, CoCo. I wanted us to have privacy so we can figure things out."

"Figure things out…you mean there's still a chance for us?"

"Hell no! My brother doesn't wanna fuck wit' you no more."

"Nichelle…please. This is a private matter between me and my fiancé." Nichelle frowned at her brother but she knew what was up.

"I advise you to listen to your brother. You're new to this. What Genesis and I share goes way back and is much deeper than you know."

"CoCo's right."

"Fine, I'll go. But call me and let me know you're okay."

"I will."

"Nichelle, I truly love your brother. He'll be fine." Nichelle didn't even acknowledge what CoCo said. She grabbed her purse and left. There was complete silence until they heard the door shut. "Genesis, you know everything I've ever done is because I love you."

"I know you believe that."

"It's true. I know how much you loved Talisa but I'll be a better wife to you than she could've ever been. And Amir loves me and I love him too. And I'm sorry about Nichelle but honestly I didn't really think she was your sister. I was just trying to get Arnez out of our lives once and for all. You know how insane he was."

"I believe we can salvage this and make it right."

"I knew that you loved me," CoCo said putting down her purse and gun to hug Genesis. "Baby, I really am the only woman for you."

"If you say so," Genesis said leaning close to CoCo's ear and whispering, "but I believe Talisa would've disagreed."

He then grabbed CoCo by the jaw and broke her neck, letting her lifeless body fall to the floor.

The next day when Genesis and Nichelle arrived at the Washington's sprawling estate, they were both excited about seeing Amir. During their ride, Genesis told Nichelle all sorts of funny stories about his son and what she had to look forward to since she would be helping Renny raise Elijah. Not once did Genesis mention CoCo and Nichelle didn't ask. If her brother ever wanted to share it with her, she would be there to listen although she believed she already knew what happened after she left.

"Are you ready?" Genesis asked when they got out the car and was walking towards the front door.

"Yes! I'm excited and nervous. I got a brother and a nephew all at the same time, how lucky am I!"

"Genesis, and you must be, Nichelle. It's wonderful to meet you," Mrs. Washington said, giving them both a hug.

"Thank you, it's wonderful to meet you too. You have such a beautiful home."

"Well your family so you consider it home too."

"You're too kind. So where's my nephew?"

"He's out in the backyard playing. Come on, I'll take you back there." Nichelle followed Mrs. Washington and Genesis stayed behind when he saw Mr. Washington coming down the stairs.

"Genesis, my wife told me that you've reunited with your sister. I'm happy for you."

"Thank you, Jeffrey. I have some news to share that I

hope will bring you some sense of happiness too."

"There is only one thing you can tell me that would do that."

"The murder of your daughter and my wife has been avenged."

"Genesis, I didn't think I would ever hear those words come out your mouth."

"I know you had your doubts and I'm glad I can finally put those doubts to rest. We'll never get Talisa back but the people who are responsible for taking her away from us have now been erased."

"Thank you," Jeffrey said shaking Genesis' hand. "When it's my time to go, it will now be in peace."

Precious was sitting in bed watching CNN on the flat screen television. The last few weeks had been difficult for her and Supreme but once again they were able to come through the storm stronger than ever. After he promised to abandon any attempt on ending Nico's life and discussed all the issues that had plagued their marriage they were now more in love than ever.

"Baby, you were supposed to be here hours ago," she said putting the television on mute.

"Sorry, babe, but this new artist I got is a handful. Is everything okay?"

"Everything is better than okay, especially since I'm pregnant." Supreme's face lit up like the Christmas tree at Rockefeller Center.

"Are you sure?"

"Positive! I took the home test and I went to the doctor. We're having a baby!"

"Damn, I love you," Supreme yelled lifting Precious off the bed and into his arms.

"Baby, wait a minute…isn't that Maya on TV." Precious grabbed the television and turned up the volume.

"That can't be true," Supreme said, putting Precious down.

"Maya's conviction has been overturned and she's going to be released on bail pending her new trial. What the fuck!"

"Precious, calm down. You're pregnant and I don't want you getting upset. I'll handle this."

"I guess Quentin made his choice and it damn sure wasn't me."

"Fuck Quentin and Maya, you got me. If he knew what was best for his daughter, he would make sure she stays behind bars. But that's okay. They'll learn the hard way."

Precious stared at Supreme and could read the thoughts going through his head and none of it was good. But Supreme was her husband and whatever he decided to do she would not only back him up but be right by his side. They were a family and the only people she cared about protecting were him, the baby growing inside of her and Aaliyah.

Epilogue
The Future

Aaliyah

Ring…ring…ring

"Hello."

"Mommy, it's me, Aaliyah." Precious glanced over at the clock to see what time it was.

"Where are you and why are you calling so late?" Precious wanted to know trying to snap out of her sleep.

"I've gotten myself in a bit of a situation."

"What sort of situation? And where are Amir and Justina? I thought you were supposed to be with them tonight?"

"I am…I mean I was but something came up."

"Cut the bullshit, Aaliyah. What the hell is going on?"

"I'm in jail and I need you to come get me out."

"Jail!" Precious screamed it out so loud that it awoke Supreme from his sleep. "You're in jail!"

"Yes. And could you please not yell. I already have a migraine headache as it is."

"Aaliyah, what are they charging you with?" Precious

asked. She gripped the phone trying to stop herself from wanting to reach through it and snatch her daughter up.

"First Degree Murder."

A KING PRODUCTION
SUPREME
MEN OF THE BITCH SERIES
JOY DEJA KING

Chapter One

I Will Be King

From my very first recollection as a kid, I re-member staring my parents directly in their eyes while sitting at the dinner table and stating with-out hesitation, "I will be king." I then looked back down at my plate of food and continued to eat.

"Xavier, what did you say?" my mother questioned, seeming completely bewildered by my comment.

"I said, I'll be king," I repeated, shrugging my shoulders in a nonchalant way. Even then at the age of four or five I had this I don't give a fuck aura about myself. When I was younger, people mistook it as me being disengaged from others. When I got older, people labeled me as arrogant, but honestly it was none of the above. I just knew, I always knew, that I would be somebody great, that I would leave a legacy that my children and grandchildren would admire and respect.

"Boy, what are you talking about now?" My dad chuckled, glancing over at my mother. "You always talking crazy. I tell you what you gon' be... a damn comedian." He laughed. My dad didn't mean any harm, he just didn't know any better.

I didn't even respond to my dad. Once again I shrugged my shoulders and continued eating my dinner. At that time, I wasn't sure the path in life I would take that would make me king. I was only sure that greatness awaited me and I was looking forward to taking my spot on the throne.

"Only one more week of school and then summer vacation... yes!" I shouted, pumping my fist in the air.

"It ain't gonna be no vacation for me. I have to go to summer school," my friend, Isaac, complained as we walked home from school.

"I still don't understand how you flunking classes in the 8th grade. I mean we don't even do shit," I said, shaking my head.

"Whatever, Xavier. Everybody can't be a fuckin' genius like you. You don't even have to open a book and already know all the answers. You've always been that way," Isaac huffed, shaking his head.

"You got excuses for everything." I shrugged, quickly losing interest in the conversation because my thirteen-year-old eyes were fixated on the lyrical battle taking place right in front of me. There was a small crowd surrounding the guys who looked to be only a few years older than me. As I walked closer, not only was I able to witness but I could hear them spitting lyrics back and forth to each other. It was a word battle that I had never seen before and the more the verbiage escalated the more intrigued I became.

"Xavier, come on! We need to get home," I heard Isaac call out, but I was paying him no mind. I wanted in on the battle. It was crazy. I had never rapped a lyric a day in my life, but hearing these two young guys who looked just like me, going at it had me mesmerized. Yeah, I had watched rappers on television and heard them on the radio, but being so up close and personal had this profound affect on me.

"Yo, Xavier we need to go!" Isaac yelled, grabbing my arm. "You know I'm on punishment. My moms told me I betta come straight home after school. So let's go or I'ma get in trouble," Isaac complained.

"Man, stop yo' whining. Besides, you on punishment... not me. Take yo' ass home. I'ma stay here and watch this rap battle," I said dropping my book bag. I was ready to make this corner block my home for the rest of the afternoon.

"Yo' you buggin'! I thought you were gon' come to my house and keep me company. My mom said you the only friend I can have over."

"Go 'head." I waved my hand, signaling Isaac to keep it moving. "I'll be over there in a minute."

Isaac glanced at me and then the two guys rapping. "Why you so interested in what they doing?" he questioned, not able to hide his confusion. It was written all over his face.

"'Cause they doing what I'ma do." I nodded my head with confidence.

"And what's that... run yo' mouth? You already know how to do that."

"Nah, dummy!" I shook my head. "I'ma be a rapper."

Isaac fell out laughing. He bent over, dropping his book bag, making this major production like he heard the funniest joke ever. "X, you got mad jokes. So you gon' be on the corner like these two clowns and call yo'self a rapper," he sneered. Isaac was now holding his stomach like he was laughing so hard that he had stomach cramps or something.

"Go 'head... keep laughing." I chuckled. "Wait and see. Not only am I gonna be a rapper. But the streets gon' say I was wanna the best that ever did it. I'ma be a star." Then I paused for a second before continuing. "Fuck a star. I'ma be a superstar." I smiled looking towards the clouds, seeing my vision up in the blue sky."

"Yo, you have officially lost yo' mind," Isaac snorted. "When you get yo' head up outta those clouds, stop by the crib. I'll be waiting on you so we can play some video games."

"Cool." I nodded as Isaac hurried off, but I never made it to his crib that day. I stayed on the block like my shoes were glued to the cement. That afternoon, on a sunny day in Queens, New York, I realized just how I would create my legacy. "Get ready world, 'cause I will be king," I mumbled under my breath as I continued to study the two young men who had become my inspiration.

P.O. Box 912
Collierville, TN 38027

A KING PRODUCTION

www.joydejaking.com
www.twitter.com/joydejaking

ORDER FORM

Name:

Address:

City/State:

Zip:

QUANTITY	TITLES	PRICE	TOTAL
	Bitch	$15.00	
	Bitch Reloaded	$15.00	
	The Bitch Is Back	$15.00	
	Queen Bitch	$15.00	
	Last Bitch Standing	$15.00	
	Superstar	$15.00	
	Ride Wit' Me	$12.00	
	Ride Wit' Me Part 2	$15.00	
	Stackin' Paper	$15.00	
	Trife Life To Lavish	$15.00	
	Trife Life To Lavish II	$15.00	
	Stackin' Paper II	$15.00	
	Rich or Famous	$15.00	
	Rich or Famous Part 2	$15.00	
	Rich or Famous Part 3	$15.00	
	Bitch A New Beginning	$15.00	
	Mafia Princess Part 1	$15.00	
	Mafia Princess Part 2	$15.00	
	Mafia Princess Part 3	$15.00	
	Mafia Princess Part 4	$15.00	
	Mafia Princess Part 5	$15.00	
	Boss Bitch	$15.00	
	Baller Bitches Vol. 1	$15.00	
	Baller Bitches Vol. 2	$15.00	
	Baller Bitches Vol. 3	$15.00	
	Bad Bitch	$15.00	
	Still The Baddest Bitch	$15.00	
	Power	$15.00	
	Power Part 2	$15.00	
	Drake	$15.00	
	Drake Part 2	$15.00	
	Female Hustler	$15.00	
	Female Hustler Part 2	$15.00	
	Female Hustler Part 3	$15.00	
	Female Hustler Part 4	$15.00	
	Female Hustler Part 5	$15.00	
	Female Hustler Part 6	$15.00	
	Princess Fever "Birthday Bash"	$6.00	
	Nico Carter The Men Of The Bitch Series	$15.00	
	Bitch The Beginning Of The End	$15.00	
	Supreme...Men Of The Bitch Series	$15.00	
	Bitch The Final Chapter	$15.00	
	Stackin' Paper III	$15.00	
	Men Of The Bitch Series And The Women Who Love Them	$15.00	
	Coke Like The 80s	$15.00	
	Baller Bitches The Reunion Vol. 4	$15.00	
	Stackin' Paper IV	$15.00	
	The Legacy	$15.00	
	Lovin' Thy Enemy	$15.00	
	Stackin' Paper V	$15.00	
	The Legacy Part 2	$15.00	
	Assassins - Episode 1	$11.00	
	Assassins - Episode 2	$11.00	
	Assassins - Episode 2	$11.00	
	Bitch Chronicles	$40.00	
	So Hood So Rich	$15.00	
	Stackin' Paper VI	$15.00	
	Female Hustler Part 7	$15.00	
	Toxic...	$6.00	

Shipping/Handling (Via Priority Mail) $8.95 1-3 Books, $16.25 4-7 Books. For 7 or more $21.50.
Total: $_____ **FORMS OF ACCEPTED PAYMENTS:** Certified or government issued checks and money Orders, all mail in orders take 5-7 Business days to be delivered

CPSIA information can be obtained
at www.ICGtesting.com
Printed in the USA
LVHW100706071022
730138LV00004BA/90